"Sam D'Allesan[dro] fiction, in the [...] anyone's I've eve[r ...] icon status, and now, years later, the work still holds up—its purity and its power still stun, like jewels in a tomb. We all make up our own legends as we go along, but Sam had only to look inside to find the divine."
—Dodie Bellamy,
        author of *Pink Steam*

"*The Wild Creatures* is enough to give anyone a crush on Sam D'Allesandro. His voice is beguilingly intimate, but never gossipy or confessional—perfect for his spare, focused little stories. He describes relationships with an attention to emotional nuance that makes his characters seem both unique and eerily familiar. His thoughts glimmer with a lucid, unsentimental intelligence and freshness. This is what queer literature looks like freed from pretension and banality."
—Alvin Orloff,
        author of *Gutter Boys*

"For years I've scoured used book stores for copies of Sam D'Allesandro's work, buying up what I could find and passing it on to friends with the injunction: Read this. *The Wild Creatures* is more than the resuscitation of a brilliant, out-of-print writer. It's that rarest of things: a true literary event."
—K.M. Soehnlein,
        author of *You Can Say You Knew Me When*

"Sam D'Allesandro's writing is like crying and then taking a nap, or taking a nap and then crying."
—Mattilda a.k.a. Matt Bernstein Sycamore,
        author of *Pulling Taffy*

The
Wild
Creatures

**Collected Stories
of Sam D'Allesandro**

The
Wild
Creatures

**Collected Stories
of Sam D'Allesandro**

**edited by
Kevin Killian**

suspect thoughts press
www.suspectthoughtspress.com

Copyright © 2005 by Kevin Killian for the literary estate of Sam D'Allesandro

Sam D'Allesandro photograph courtesy of his literary estate
Kevin Killian photograph by Loring McAlpin
Cover image and design by Shane Luitjens/Torquere Creative
Book design by Greg Wharton/Suspect Thoughts Press

First Edition: August 2005
10 9 8 7 6 5 4 3 2 1

Library of Congress Cataloging-in-Publication Data

D'Allesandro, Sam.
   The wild creatures : collected stories of Sam D'Allesandro/ edited by Kevin Killian.
      p. cm.
   ISBN-13: 978-0-9763411-1-6 (pbk.)
   ISBN-10: 0-9763411-1-5 (pbk.)
   1. Gay men--Fiction. I. Killian, Kevin. II. Title.

PS3554.A4357A6 2005
813'.54--dc22

                                        2005019468

Suspect Thoughts Press
2215-R Market Street, #544, San Francisco, CA 94114-1612
www.suspectthoughtspress.com

Contents

Introduction

Sam D'Allesandro wasn't his real name—he wore that ironic badge of identity with a disarming, take-it-or-leave-it grin—but it wasn't until after he died that I found out he had been born Richard Anderson. Surely the plainest name of an American author, ever? At his Hugo Street apartment, after his funeral, as parents and family showed us pictures of him growing up on the farm, and so forth, they kept talking about "Richard" this and "Richard" that, and I must have looked bewildered enough that Fritz Schultz took me aside and whispered, "Sam's real name was Richard." Last month Sean Monohan showed me a series of drivers' licenses he keeps in a box, more pictures of Sam, with the name Richard Anderson eventually dying out, circa age twenty-three. And the name "Sam D'Allesandro" taking over, supplanting the birth-name, the other discarded names. And always the photos on the licenses radiant and luscious—he might have been modeling for Bruce Weber. So that when he decided to try to model and for some reason no photographer could really capture his beauty, he was disappointed, of course. It's odd that there are people who are counter-photogenic, who look better in life than on film.

With a stricken look, Sam would confide that he had been born the son of the '70s Warhol superstar Joe Dallesandro, and I believed him, though something about the chronology didn't gibe. Later on, in Los Angeles, this claim backfired when a press listing of a reading he gave at Beyond Baroque, the nonprofit arts center in Venice, alluded to this famous dad and the phone rang and Benjamin Weissman picked up the phone. Who knew that the real Joe lived a few miles away, very much alive, very much ready to chew poor

9

Sam D'Allesandro

Ben a new asshole? Uh-oh! Maybe Sam identified with Joe Dallesandro's working-class values, his diamond-in-the-rough appeal, his "teenage integrity," or his sheer sex allure? Joe played the addict, the hustler, the stud, the ambisexual whose lack of affect had its own powerful effect—Sam did too.

When one met Sam, he proffered this fake name as if only he and you were in on the joke, as a shortcut to intimacy. Another part of him wanted to be famous, so he could get to meet and know as equals his idols—Patti Smith, Yoko Ono, Jean Genet, Andy Warhol, James Baldwin, Laura Nyro, Willem de Kooning, Dory Previn, David Bowie, Nina Simone, William Burroughs, Bob Dylan, Kathy Acker, Brian Eno, Leonard Cohen. Did he ever meet any of them? I don't believe he did, but such was his tact that I don't really know. The dedication of *Slippery Sins* (Sam's 1983 book of poetry) reads "This is for Fritz and for Patti." Over the Internet, I once bought a copy of *Slippery Sins* that Sam had inscribed to Yoko Ono—"I've been wishing you love for fifteen years"—but she must get hundreds of fanboy books a year. I wonder.

But anyway, he did get to meet us—the prose writers of San Francisco who were busy working on a "New Narrative," a community-based project in which we hoped to recuperate narrative from the trap of modernism by rearticulating it as a postmodern conceptual art, wise to the precepts of Language poetry. We took Sam to our hearts, and learned of his potential quick, thanks to the untiring efforts of the late Steve Abbott, who was the real live wire, who always knew which way the wind was blowing. Immediately Sam took up the pose of a besieged Nijinsky fending off the imperious advances of Diaghilev. (Steve, Sam told us, wanted to spank his ass with a slab of bacon. And you know, it did sort of sound like something Steve would want to do.) Yet Sam depended on Steve, and took to his teenage daughter

10

The Wild Creatures

Alysia as well. After Sam's death, Steve did a thoughtful job of editing *The Zombie Pit* for Crossing Press (1989), when they had a brief fling with publishing "gay fiction." It's been out of print for nearly fifteen years and Sam's executors, myself among them, are supergrateful to Suspect Thoughts Press for picking up the slack and to you, of course, for reading this new edition.

I first met Sam in the late summer of 1983, when Bryan Monte introduced me to him after their reading at Intersection, in those days a top artist-run space in San Francisco. Sam's book *Slippery Sins* had appeared, and its potential intrigued me although I disliked the poetry. That is, it seemed like performance poetry. Later, he said he had taken the performance texts he had written and performed, and chopped them up so they'd look like poetry, but he'd also written some "real" poems. Over the years, with the encouragement of his longtime friend and former lover Fritz Schultz, Sam's work grew in power and authority. If the too-beautiful poems of *Slippery Sins* were vague about sex, vague about gender and class, the prose he started to write now broke these boundaries down—flattened them out, in a series of bulldozing maneuvers, risky with their enormity. His writing became "edgy," edgy enough to match his personality. And his willingness to revise, his attempts to improve every sentence, became clear.

He would rewrite a paragraph endlessly, often with mixed results. Even if it was "perfect," he might throw it away. I imagine he did the same thing with his attitudes, his feelings, with the various lives he led. This creation, revision, perfection, and dismissal links his work in a mysterious way to God's, or what I imagine is God's. His stories attempt a religious philosophy they don't achieve, for what actuates them is his own desire, then its absence. His book comes to us as a phallocentric model of writing, the power and the exhaustion endlessly

11

Sam D'Allesandro

renewable. It's no accident, I suppose, that each story seemed less like a rewrite of his last than a mirror image of it. "In my work," he wrote, "I am not wanting to add to something or generate more, rather I am stripping the subject down to its itsness...a core, that which is beyond a surface, the core from which the surface emanates." Like the director Robert Bresson, he had no use for characters per se; he preferred "models."

Some Textual Notes

"Nothing Ever Just Disappears" appeared in the third issue of *No Apologies*, which I edited as Bryan Monte's guest. George Stambolian read it there and asked for Sam's address, eventually securing its reprint for his influential anthology *Men on Men* (New American Library, 1986). When Bryan moved to the East Coast, I began a magazine called *Mirage* and invited Sam to contribute a story. He sent me "Electrical Type of Thing," which he envisaged as a counterpart to Dennis Cooper's "My Mark" and Bob Glück's "Sex Story." The following issue of *Mirage* was dedicated to the Black Mountain poet John Wieners, and after studying Wieners' early masterpiece *The Hotel Wentley Poems* (1958), Sam channeled John Wieners' mournful energy into "All I Want Is to Die Famous," a lurid exposé of the last days of the starlet Carol Wayne.

At this point Sam's work became more complex and ambitious (and lengthy). After rejection by several other magazines, "My Day with Judy" appeared in the third issue of *Mirage*. In the last year of Sam's life, his story "Jane and Sam" was published in *Yellow Silk,* and a condensed version of "The Zombie Pit" appeared in *Zyzzyva*.

Sam and I met only rarely. I retain, however, an indelible picture of his looks, reinforced by the skill with which he was able to make them one of the central

The Wild Creatures

themes of his writing. I've known three or four writers with more glamour, and two or three with more sex appeal—but Sam's personal beauty was astonishing. At first it formed a screen behind which one could hardly see his work. One afternoon he came over to visit and we watched the John Huston film *Reflections in a Golden Eye*. Elizabeth Taylor and Marlon Brando. (On a then-new VCR; funny to think they're so ubiquitous now, but back then people would make dates to see one.) In a just world, I thought, Taylor and Brando would be sitting in my living room watching Sam and me on the screen. We decided to collaborate on a story, "My Fine Feat Hered Friend," which began with great gusto and then it sort of petered out, as you'll see.

Dodie Bellamy and Sam exchanged a series of letters under the aliases "Mina Harker" and "Sam X," and years later Dodie published both sides of the correspondence in a book called *Real: The Letters of Mina Harker and Sam D'Allesandro* (Talisman House, 1994, and still in print), together with Sam's very last story, "Travels with My Mother," which Dodie painstakingly transcribed from an audio cassette made two months before his death. Dodie wrote:

> In this piece we get to hear the writer's process, constructing a fiction out of available facts and time. The tape is spliced often, as the voice breaks in with new, undeveloped thought, always to improve the story, to take it in new directions, to reveal or confine or conflate—I've surrounded these breaks with parentheses for clarity. Thus there's a "you" in the story unlike the usual second person, a heroic "you" hounded both by HIV and by the narrative imperative. Although AIDS isn't mentioned in "Travels with My Mother," it haunts the piece like a revenant, right down to the sudden faint

13

Sam D'Allesandro

that "ends" the story in a comic shadow of death
itself. The story impinges on itself, as I imagine
the virus impinges on the subject of the body.
(61)

The tape is hard to listen to, and try to imagine as
you read it that he is producing it for you breath by
breath, fainter and fainter, and then it ends, tape hissing,
no more voice, no voice left.

When Steve Abbott edited *The Zombie Pit,* he collected the six stories previously published in periodicals,
and printed for the first time the brief pieces "Lenny,"
"1960," "Walking to the Ocean This Morning," the
travelogue "14 Days," and a version of the unfinished
novella, "Giovanni's Apartment."

Basically the present volume contains all the stories
of *The Zombie Pit,* plus "Travels with My Mother" from
Real, and adds the prose versions of a few pieces Sam
had published earlier, with line breaks somewhat
arbitrarily inserted, to turn them into "poems," in his
book of poetry *Slippery Sins* — "Jimmy," "Speedboys,"
and "The Wild Creatures."

I worked from the manuscripts in Sam's archive,
which Sean Monohan made available to me. Out of the
notebooks, I transcribed a few more stories — the brief
"Teddy Kennedy," and the coming-of-age memoir slash
fiction "How I Came to Dinosaur Pond," and "our"
story, "A Fine Feat Hered Friend." There's also a
marvelous dream journal which I don't print here,
because, well, it's not really story material. I wanted just
one book with all the stories in it, and this is the one for
me.

Personally I took great interest in Sam's development
because it seemed to me, at that time, that we were
experiencing another "San Francisco Renaissance," new
narrative subdivision. My own work seemed inextri-

The Wild Creatures

cably tied to that of Bob Glück, Bruce Boone, Dodie Bellamy, Sam D'Allesandro, Steve Abbott, Carla Harryman, Francesca Rosa, Marsha Campbell, Camille Roy, and a bit afield Kathy Acker, Dennis Cooper, Brad Gooch, and many others. We were all in this "thing" together. It was like a physical element, a fog, or a thicket. Or like *Soup*, the name of Steve Abbott's New Narrative magazine. I can hardly expand on that any further without getting sentimental.

The last year of Sam's life I never saw him, once; as his beauty crumbled and the facial wasting set in, he became a recluse, methodically trying to finish his last pieces. I worked out later that he just plain didn't want to be seen. Finally, in an abrupt change of policy, Sam agreed to see the photographer Robert Giard, who brought his camera into the darkened apartment and took the photos of Sam, all emaciated and rickety, that years later appeared in Giard's book, *Particular Voices: Portraits of Gay and Lesbian Writers* (MIT Press, 1998). When he got sick, Sam wrote in a letter to me:

> I'm terminal and that seems to make me important, no longer answerable for my bills or attitudes; my refused meals a sign of increasing power; withdrawal, a symptom of bravery. No one will say so, but I'm terminal. I don't care about politics or the old lovers I'd wanted to see on my deathbed. I've forgotten the meaning of everything except my medication. Buried beneath layers of thin tissue, a refugee on a field of darkness, I am isolated, confused, as white noise fills my ears. Only the world inside my imploding body is real, like watching on film as I disintegrate. I clap my hands at this new game that already bores me. I'm a pumpkin caving in, in a tunnel without return that grows narrower all the time.

Nothing Ever Just Disappears

1.

I didn't know exactly what he meant by "accessible." He said he liked people who were, because he wasn't. He said a lot of things that I didn't exactly understand, or that seemed to carry connotations other than those most obvious. Or then again maybe they didn't. And often I would have asked for more information, explanation... intent, if he had been someone else saying the same thing. I didn't want to know him as much as I wanted to be able to be around my image of him. I didn't want things to get too difficult. I wanted to continue to be uncertain about him for as long as possible—to sustain the way it is with meeting someone new before a more thorough understanding brings comfort into the relationship. I did not want comfort. I did want to be comfortable with not seeking comfort or predictability in him. I wanted to be challenged but not in pain. All of these thoughts came to me some weeks after our first meeting.

I met him at the cigarette store. We just started talking. He seemed aimless, but not confused; unhurried but not unscheduled—we went to the park to see the ducks. We talked and smoked, smoked and talked. In fact, he talked to me more than most of my friends do. That attracted me. He was interested in me, and that interested me. Here's what I found out that afternoon: He was a painter. He was a waiter. He was thirty. It was enough to know. We talked about other things: observations, an irritating little girl that kept screaming and splashing her mother, the duck with one leg, the cherry trees...they were in bloom. Later, on the street, he told me he'd had a good time. I took his number, it started raining, and we both went home.

"Do you go out much?"
    "Not much."
    "Where do you go?"
    "Nowhere special."
    "Do you like to dance?"
    "Yes, but I don't like the dance places."
    "I know what you mean. Sometimes you have to forget your dislike of them so you can go and have a good time."
    "I know what you mean."
    "I like small things, that's where my pleasure comes from. The big things disappoint me, but there is always something small to enjoy for a moment, to look to for keeping life pleasurable. I like these cigarettes. I like a beer. I like the park."
    "Sure, but it sounds like you're afraid to make yourself vulnerable to disappointment, so you miss the big things—it could make your life flat. I understand what you mean, but I think it's a mistake."
    "Maybe so, but then I'm not committed to living correctly at the moment either. It's hard for me to think about wasting my life when the alternatives don't seem much less wasteful. The way I see it, we're all just doing things anyway. I'm not sure I think it matters so much how they're done."
    "I know what you mean. I think it does matter, but I'm not sure how. Your way is not bad. I do the same thing. We're the same."
    "No, we're not."
    "Maybe you're right."

In his apartment I always became very relaxed. I didn't do a lot of thinking there. When I entered, I stopped making plans, worrying, noting the little disappointments and triumphs of the day. Sometimes I would walk

Sam D'Allesandro

around the rooms while he was shaving or when I was there alone and just look at things I had seen before. Nothing seemed to really have a permanent location. The things that were scattered looked good wherever they had fallen anyway: books (serious books), magazines (frivolous magazines), canvases, cups, ashtrays, cigarette boxes, shoes and pens and brushes and tablets—a generally more attractive class of scatter than I found at many places of similar disorganization. The living room had good light. The bedroom had curtains covered with layers and layers of thick paint, so that they resembled something out of *The Flintstones* where all the furniture is made of stone, even something seemingly pliable, like curtains. It made the bedroom seem like a cave. Artists do lots of things like that.

In some ways being there was like taking a nap for me. It was a pleasant experience, even though elsewhere I would have been bored. It was not uncommon, at times, for us both to sit in silence—smoking—as if just being in the same room was as fine a way of visiting as another. But of course it wasn't always this way.

When I was with him I did a lot of sliding through the environments I found myself in: slipping through the air, exploring without paying much attention to the subject, sitting as if waiting but without thought of for what. Something more than hanging out but less than participating—that's what I was doing, or not doing, that's what was happening to me. And because this happened around him, it all seemed interesting. Away from him I was more productive, stimulated and stimulating, both volatile and quick to laugh—I had always been so—but around him things changed. The air got thicker. It seemed like an effort to do anything quickly, so I didn't and liked not doing so. He was a drug: a nice, soft, furry tranquilizer. And all of this was what I needed.

The Wild Creatures

One day something lousy happened to me. Here's how we talked about it:

S: I was anxious, now I'm nervous—I can't stop thinking about it...

J: Don't try so hard. Problems have a life of their own.

S: Yeah, but I want to forget this so I can go on to something else. I have more important things to be obsessed with. Okay, this is it, I'm completely putting it out of my head. Let's just forget about it...

J: Okay. What do you want for dinner?

S: I mean, let's just not worry about it. It's no big deal. I've done it, I've been through it, I'm sick of it. Let's just not think about it.

J: Right.

S: I mean what can you say? It's like so many things that happen: I didn't like it, I gave it a chance, now I still don't like it.

J: Sure.

S: It's now, it's modern, it's dead. I think I'm starting to let go of it.

J: Yeah. I mean, to me it's always like the way everything I thought I would want to do twice turned out to be more than enough once.

S: Right.

J: How can we always be cool when we live in fear? Everything, really, is coated to some extent with a layer of anxiety...and that's not always bad, but still...

S: Exactly. It's a given we tend to discount.

J: Yeah, you can't really work too much with that one.

S: You're right. Okay, what should we have for dinner?

J: ...You did it, you saw it, you're sick of it...

19

Sam D'Allesandro

S: Right.

J: I mean, it was now, now it's dead so...you know...

S: Let it dissipate.

J: Right.

S: Right.

J: What's for dinner?

My god, we've become symbiotic, I thought. It was a small shock. It was in conflict with the uncertainty I'd always valued in us. It had been a long time since I felt like I was floating. My tranquilizer was becoming more real, more multifaceted, more demanding. I knew that would happen, it always happens; but I can never quite tell the moment it begins. If I could, maybe I could head it off at the pass, keep things vague. But that didn't turn out to be what I wanted after all. Even vagueness has its limitations. I don't know if there was a moment when I decided to let go and fall into the relationship, or if I didn't notice when such a moment could have occurred because I was already falling. I've never been one to take responsibility for everything that happens to me, so that makes it hard to always know whether a decision is a conscious one or not. After all, there is such a thing as the tyranny of fate. There is a feeling of falling...

2.

What happened in the middle and the end are what stand out for me. I guess the middle is what drops out of a lot of our memories. The end points often define what we remember of what happens between them. So I'm skipping most of the middle part. Let's just say things were fine. Some usual things happened, some unusual. That's normal. We weren't too interested in things being perfect and they weren't. We learned from each other. We were starting to have dreams together, but they didn't happen, they stayed dreams. Then everything changed.

3.

When the time came I wasn't waiting for him to die. I didn't wait. I wasn't really able to think about what was happening. I didn't think. I was just there. I got used to the sight of the tubes that sucked at his arms like hungry little snakes, trying to put the life back in. And I got used to hearing my existential baby, my nice, soft, furry tranquilizer, talked about like a textbook experiment. It was sometimes hard to trust that I was awake, that what was happening was what was happening. When I went in to see him for the last time it didn't feel like a last anything. At least not at the time. Later those moments, what happened in them and what didn't, would always stand out.

I don't remember driving home. I unlocked the door and closed all the windows. I took a bath. I sat. I listened to the phone ring. I went to bed. It was day again and then it wasn't. This happened several times. I was born, I died, and slowly the night would seep back in. Sometimes I'd reach out as if to touch his face in the dark so I'd know I wasn't alone.

Later I made the calls. I tried not to listen to the people on the other end. I'd already said all of the things anyone else could say. After a while I just dialed the numbers, said my lines, and hung up. "He had to go. He's gone. I'm sorry. Goodbye."

When it happens, it's like the film broke in midreel; you don't expect it and you're still expecting everything you were before. Everything in my life except me was suddenly different. Eventually that would make me different too, but it takes a while to catch up. Someone said the pain would go away, but I'm not sure that's where I want it to go. It's how I feel him most sharply.

Sam D'Allesandro

Without it, every move I make echoes because he's not there to absorb me. I don't like bouncing back at myself. A dead lover wants your soul, wants your life, and then your death too. And you give it, it's the only way to feel anything again. Take the death as a lover and sleep with it and eat it and purge it and suck it back in quick. And finally it's no event, it's nothing that happened, it's just you: an anger and a beauty that never really goes away. Not something you can wait out as it disappears, nothing ever really just disappears.

Everything's okay now. I'm not waiting for anything. I shave and I comb my hair every morning. I look fine. Nothing about me looks different. I change the sheets. I do the dishes. I pay the bills. Just like before.

Everything's okay. I spelled out his name with trash on the beach, poured the gasoline, and lit it up. Pretty, but he didn't come back.

I'm okay. I was thinking: *We were fine – some usual things happened, some unusual. That's normal.* I wonder if there was a moment when he decided to let go and fall into it, or if he didn't notice when such a moment could have occurred because he was already falling. We can't take responsibility for everything that happens to us. After all, there is such a thing as the tyranny of fate. I had wanted to be comfortable with not seeking comfort. I had wanted to be challenged, but not in pain. I guess a lot of things seem to carry connotations other than those most obvious.

I went to the grocery store and bought everything frozen. Except for the freezer the refrigerator's empty. So I've been keeping the film for his next project in there. It looks really clean with just the yellow and black boxes against the white.

The Wild Creatures

1.

It's a kind of cold, north-state rain, a fat, too-high-into-the-foothills rain, threatening to thicken into snow. It makes me dig deeper into the quilts — those huge, faithful, goosey wombs, ready to warm the coldest of winters or souls. The overhead bulb suddenly and cleanly blasts an intense artificial morning into my den. The quilts rip away and, as my eyes strain to once again begin their function, I hear my father's voice, loud and familiar, telling me to hurry — get up, let's go! — but it's not morning yet, something is not right, clearly and urgently.

An old ewe too fat and dumbly obstinate had made a poor choice, if she chose at all, lambing early and badly in the storm. Twins. On the other side of the swollen creek. Barely born lamb-angels, soaked and weakened, needing a chance that only the warmth even a rickety shed like ours might offer, where mother's tongue can lick the sticky birth covering from the little ice-cube bodies, and hay and the amber glow of headlamps can cover them in musty, insulating layers.

Into an old coat, rubber boots, battered cowboy hat stained from other, similar nights, I trod out with flashlights through a sponge of waterlogged land, past a sinking stretch where the noisy suction of the mud pulls against my legs and the anchoring boots, into fields running wild with new rivulets. We make our way through blackness, from one familiar landmark to another: the fig trees where boys my age carved initials a hundred years ago; the dark mark of the spring that will serve as lifeline to the wild creatures (and my salvation when the summer comes on 100 degrees worth) — now

23

Sam D'Allesandro

just a black hole of a restless La Brea waiting patiently for the offering of careless farm animals; and on, until finally we reach the crossing log, just long enough to bridge the creek in a narrow spot.

The water is now even with the log's once-elevated stature. In the slowly easing black I can see the ewe, enormous and heavy, her long wool soaked and its water-repellency long surrendered. And she is down—where no ewe mother ever is unless she can't get up. She doesn't bleat—this is not a children's story—but rather she stares up at us, near death, dumb and miserable, as she tries to use her breath to warm the babies. One can raise a head, the other not even that. Now timing is everything. We have a mission, my father and I, and even with odds against us we must try. Life here, especially here, where it is so often seen in its newness, is often important, always demanding. We do not let it slip away while there is still even the smallest chance for survival. Here we survive on such chances.

My father scoops up the lambs in a bunch, the long four-battery flashlight awkwardly poking like a stamen through the soft bouquet of gray. At forty-nine, he's recovering from spinal fusion so I alone must do the pushing and lifting. Levering the inflated ewe to useless legs, I try to force a lock into the hinge of knees so that I can keep her trembling upright. One hand under the chin, the other lost deep into the matted wool of her rump, she stands, using me as her shaky will and foundation. And we move. I propel us inch by inch. The swollen creek is sassy and giddy with new power, the crossing log too small for my heavy cargo. So we must ford the current, plunging into the ice cold, praying she doesn't pull us both down to the river stones when we reach the deafening center. With the enormous breath of the choiceless we are into it, in one motion, before either of us has time to think about what's happening, sloshing and slashing and cussing our way through, jostling for

24

The Wild Creatures

invisible footholds in the slippery rocks, reaching for a solidity and strength not yet existing in my skinny twelve years, and getting it, in the fast kick of a new adrenaline rush, blood jumping, muscles sprinting, mind stupid, and fearless; heart bouncing like mad against the thin wall of my chest, breath heaving and lost in the sound of the storm; ewe crazy, wild-eyed, like some woolly Medea... If she could, she would kill me. She, exhausted thing, is trying to stand and help fight the rushing war of current. Both of us give it all we've got.

We use gravity. I try to trick the storm, propelling us with such a downhill hurry that we move in a series of forward falls like dropped stones reaching the ground. We are the underdogs, Davids to the storm's Goliath, and we use anything we can, impossibly, to win. But now we are stopped. Inevitably. Here the raging will not give in. It's angry at our progress. The pressure of the current pushes harder against us.

Digging my feet into the hidden rocks below me, I make my legs into a wild and slanting wedge that props us up against the push, the damned push. Now it's a battle. The soaked ewe is heavier, like lead. Somehow I must fight harder...

And then her legs are gone, dropped like a trap door beneath her, both of us pulled into the frothy mess of fat water. Starting back in from the bank, I fight to keep our heads up, gasping, my clothes awkward. The dropped and abandoned flashlight beams up a shiver of silver white into a tree. I will not give her up, she's mine. I refuse to believe I'm in danger; all the pioneer movies I've ever seen flash through my mind...I fight to stand with the anchor of cargo, finally regain my footing, test our strength, and then slowly I begin almost invisible progress. I use the water that has nearly beaten us to help me as I half-carry, half-float her the rest of the way. My father helps us onto the bank from where we collapse in the shallow overflow, exhausted yet winning.

Sam D'Allesandro

As dawn begins, we reach the shed. Heat lamps on, hay arranged as carefully as if Baby Jesus was in our care, and maybe he is, maybe not, but whoever it is now seems more precious and redeemed. The lambs are too weak to eat on their own, and a forced feeding fails. We try a jolt of whiskey to the little hearts, have some ourselves, and finally a little milk squeezes its slippery way into the tiny bellies. Soon a straw quilt covers the thawing murmurs.

I stay home from school to nurse the lambs. One dies at midday, a decision made long before dawn, but the other will live and grow to enormity in my eyes from this tiny and tentative beginning—through docking and wormings, summers and winters, countless shearings and lambs of her own. Here in the Neverland we never really fight nature, we only try to give it a run for its money. Not because we must win, but because we must try.

2.

Taking out the long snake of a rifle, its danger beckoning to the touch, my father would set out to hunt muskrats, tramping the marshy edges of the pond like a strange and restless elephant in oversized rubber boots. He searched the water for a double line of vibrating ripples, always pointing like poison arrows to the submerged target. The story would be over if he could shoot.

Sometimes he could not, and sometimes the great blast would echo and ricochet through the startled little canyon only to signal another report of a miss. He was no hunter. The wild creatures were friends, and he taught us the same. But the muskrats ate holes in the dam, so he went: there are certain things that have to be done on a farm—even a tiny, after-five one like ours.

A skunk is in the chicken pen, weasels have the hysterically honking goose by the neck, raccoons have

The Wild Creatures

cornered our burry, too-old yellow cat—maybe deaf but now mad and screeching in the darkness like a burning banshee. Wake up, lights on, out of bed, and quickly into the noisy night in underwear, naked, no time for anything. We grab any weapon within reach: a stick, the flashlight, maybe just a shoe, as we clap and yell our frontier fury at bloody intruders.

Somehow, we who knew so little of such things, so far from the sprawling city that spawned us, had become protectors, depended on. Sweet, silly cows, cuckoo chickens, our dumb but honest sheep: they all seemed to need us much too often. Once wild dogs cornered a ewe, and before I could reach her they chewed a hole clear into her head. I chased them for miles, crying and sweating, my lungs on fire and bursting until finally I collapsed in the angry exhausted heap of a boy who tried too hard and failed.

Life isn't always fair, that's one thing learned very young on a farm. I remember my mother one early summer morning in bra and panties, a fat black deer-gun against the white, protecting the new chicks she'd waited and hoped so long for. When she came in, miserable, from her fearless brush with a skunk that won, I snapped her picture. Then we both lay down on the cool kitchen linoleum and laughed. We had come so far from anywhere we'd ever been before. And we were here to stay. We loved the wild creatures but were not to be bullied—at least not too much.

3.

Hugging the hot and gun-colored iron trestle, searing and steaming against the wetness of bodies freshly emerged from the summer pond below, we hold tight to the railing. We push as close to its surface as we can go. The old, tired wooden crossbeams beneath us wake up, bracing for the weight to be carried when they bridge the

27

path of the oncoming train over the water's dent and onto the other side. Already we can feel the trembling: ours, the trestle's, even that of the water beneath as it starts to breathe and shimmer with the approach of the rumbling. It's coming...

Tim and I hold tight. We are soldered to the musty metal, paralyzed into irretrievably chosen positions. We can't move now, this is something we must do. My father would kill me if he knew. I'm scared, it's coming, I hug the railing tighter—God, we could die so easily here. The sunbaked heads of the railing's bolts make pale-blooded dents in my belly.

And it's here! No more time for thinking: only the hot iron vibrating beneath us, the syncopated rush and roar hammering by just a foot away, jolting and threatening to pick us off our perch like matchsticks and throw us into the wake of the thundering. All sound now. All sound, all feeling...the rush and whoosh—heat of an unnatural wind, a nineteenth-century God still demonstrating a power beyond us, a power right next to us. Through the tracks I can see Linda and Rhonda perched on the crossbeams just beneath, screaming and laughing in two-piece bathing suits.

Southern Pacific, Santa Fe, Eastern...the boxcars count off as they pass by, marked by little gaps in the roaring—ninety-nine, one hundred, 1—0—1!—and just when it seems they'll go on forever, the train's gone, suddenly, as fast as it came. The silence, the absence, is deafening, as the last clicks and clacks move off into the distance. I can't move. The death grip of my hands won't let up. I've become one part of this line of iron, still tingling and shivering against me with the weight that has just passed over.

Moments fatten into gigantic segments, like boxcars barely able to pass, and when I'm sure I will never move again my body slowly begins to rise, a few inches at a time, skin red with the heat, stinging pins and needles.

The Wild Creatures

My senses reel, like stepping back into the sun after all afternoon in a black movie theater. As the weight and blur of my head slowly clears, I see Linda and Rhonda already diving and cool in the water below, their laughter beginning to bubble up through my numbed and deafened ears.

4.

Summer evenings when the light stayed longer and the heat began to lift a little, out came the plastic ball and bat. My father always wanted us all to play. And we would, for hours, long past the mosquitoes and dying twilight until it was too dark to see the fly ball, hurriedly looking for our mitts... Then inside for Oreos and TV—*Lost in Space, Gunsmoke, Lucy*—all of us in dirty summer feet, later to tuck between the wrinkled sheets.

We were not a starched-white-linen family. We were not a strict or polite family, but we were a family: some kind of restless, up-and-down, enduring family—one thing we did was endure. Endlessly. And if we weren't quite a family during my wordless leavings to empty places—nebulous times in the deadening belly of who-knows-what adolescent devil—we were one when I came back, sometimes a little shaky from wrestling myself free, but back. They always waited for me.

Mother would be home, frying in the kitchen, still in her white nurse suit, swearing at the noisy and vicious popping grease. She'd stop long enough to plant a kiss, smile, and tell me to set the damned table. Still sassy and funny, she was the same: yelling out the back for all to come in, our raucous dinner hour was about to begin. Soon my father would be there on the step, fresh and musty from checking the cows and looking at his little stamp of land. Still in his muddy jeans and rubber boots.

If he was a dreamer, he did not infect us with his dreams. He went to work and came home with an end-

Sam D'Allesandro

less sea of grocery bags, full and ready to burst like unpicked peaches. He did his favorite living at the end of the day: all the feedings and fence-mendings through dusks that came and left and always came back again, like the unending things needing to be done there. Everything returns eventually on the farm. Maybe this was the dream, a quiet picture he found and fed. Happily and knowingly, he lost himself deep inside of it.

My mother and father are the way I remember them, still patiently waiting out prodigal returns. They must know me—they should; after all, I am all their sensitivities rolled into one, all the vulnerabilities they managed to keep now raging and unleashed on the world. And as I grow older, stronger, and live my life in a different way from my brothers and sisters, they still cheer from the sidelines—confused but as proud as when my brother made touchdowns. Some things have to last, we need them to, and we will not have it any other way.

Electrical Type of Thing

"There's more to relationships than acquisition." Scott was trying to talk me out of something. I wasn't listening. I was thinking about the different ways a relationship can turn out. A lover can be a best friend, a piece of furniture, or an eternity. My Chris treated people like furniture—jumping from one to the next, rearranging the pieces, tossing out, and retrieving. Chris says that he's "a very visual person." That means he doesn't like the way a lot of people look right off the bat and quickly tires of the looks of those he does like. Visual fickleness. He moves from face to face, body to body, from inside of one asshole to inside of another. The whole process takes as little of getting to know someone as it sounds.

Chris is beautiful, handsome, sexy. That means person after person is willing to let him put his cock inside of them, or lick the sweat from his belly, or do whatever Chris decides he wants. He knows just how to do everything so that you're always ready for more. His eyes are brown and steady. Unavoidable. In a bar they look straight into yours from across the room—he's interested in getting your interest going, no matter what he plans or doesn't plan to do about it. But it's the hands you should be watching. He might slip one of them down your pants and tease your asshole while giving you a kiss. Then when your resistance is zero he might give you a nice pat and be on his way. He might. He might do anything. With Chris even a pat and a quick kiss are worth something. That's the way it is with him. And the way he does whatever he's decided to do will always seem okay. Almost respectable. He's never rude. His tone is always friendly. There's nothing you could pin down as deceptive, yet the effect is the same: left alone with your buns in the oven, or your iron in the fire, or your head up your ass. That's how I used to think of Chris. I hated him, and I would stay with him whenever he'd have me.

I've known Chris for four years now. I'm the only one that he has continued to see and that has continued to see him for that length of time. We have sex about twenty times a year. Sometimes we do it four times in a month and then don't see each other for four months. And we live in the same city. It's not so big. Usually a chance meeting gets us started. It's always up to him, he knows I'm ready. He knows I'm hooked on him. I know that if we're at the same party we'll end up together. We both know that I'm different than most of the guys he sees. We're on to each other. He wants me in a different way, but almost as much as I want him. We are drawn to each other. We are each the free electron the other's unbalanced nucleus needs. It's an electrical type of thing. A charge.

Once when I was on the other side of the country and thought we'd never be in the same city again, I sent him a card telling him he was an asshole and that I loved him. When I came back he told me he loved me too. If that were true, I wondered, then why did I get to see him so seldom? He said that I was the one who never called — then I couldn't get hold of him for a month. Still, he does want me. Just not all the time. He does want me but that doesn't mean he can be around me too much. He's just the kind of guy he is. And I'm the kind I am. Everyone that can't have him wants him. I want everyone I can't have.

Over coffee I told Scott and Jeff about the way Chris and I are together. I wanted to hear someone else accept the relationship just as it is, the way I have. Instead they gently tried to tell me about the way loving relationships are supposed to be, always sharing and sensitive, etc. Chris and I are sensitive, only in a different way. Chris

The Wild Creatures

and I share some needs and the means to satisfy them. Together we're basically self-contained. Scott and Jeff tell me that there are other needs to consider, that a relationship can't be based on sexual intensity alone. I say if sexual intensity's there the relationship has already been based.

I don't think we can always be sure what it is we need; that seems to be different for me than it is for Scott and Jeff. Or is it? Maybe Scott and Jeff have forgotten how good pure intensity can feel. Maybe they've never experienced the vulnerability of being spanked during sex by someone they really want. Or known the relief you can feel when someone gets you to forget yourself totally. Someone who helps you to find a subhuman state—no language, no questions, no problems—just a pulsing, quivering slab of sensation. People would pay a guru or a Rolfer to do that. Or Werner Erhard. It's not an unusual desire. It's not an unusual need, letting someone else take the reins once in a while. I'd rather be physically fucked by Chris than verbally fucked by Werner Erhard. I never wanted my parents to spank me, but when I can pick who's doing it I can enjoy a good spanking. Skin craves sensation. It's those nerve endings. It's the way we're made.

I wonder if protozoa ever get into a little S/M. They seem to think about sex less and do it more. They do it all the time. One-celled nymphomaniacs constantly going at it in a big way, without the aid of cockrings, lubricants, vibrators, or pornography. That can't be totally unfamiliar to us. It's basic, after all.

I don't think Scott and Jeff quite understood. I needed more of something. Self-awareness alone had become pretty vapid. Everything seemed too neat. I didn't want to be dirty exactly, but I didn't want to shave every day either. I didn't want to get hurt exactly, but I liked sex rough. I needed someone who could satisfy urges I couldn't even name. Someone compli-

33

Sam D'Allesandro

cated enough to be exciting, primal enough to be effective. For me that was Chris. He hadn't chosen his shape and I hadn't chosen mine, yet all the right barriers were there to create the charge.

I met Jack in L.A. He drove a little red truck with four-wheel drive and a Dolby stereo. At first I didn't want him but his shyness interested me. He was very young and clean. He had very hairy legs and arms and a totally smooth chest with large, sensitive nipples. His body seemed so vulnerable, so beyond his control—I could make him tremble in a second just by teasing his tits. Soon he wanted to live in my asshole. If I was standing naked anywhere, like brushing my teeth or shaving, he'd come out of nowhere and have his face between my legs, kissing my cheeks and licking my asshole. He was obsessed. I never stopped him. It seemed like his right. It was so easy to give him so much pleasure.

Sometimes he wanted me to spank him and then fuck him once his ass was all red. He'd whimper all the way through it. I could tell it hurt him to be fucked, but he wanted it anyway. I respected his willingness to be hurt a little. He'd dumped his conditioning of not being able to want anything that hurts. It was a spiritualness with him, not a sickness. A respect for his own desires without questioning their right to exist. He was perfect, because he had no guilt.

Some people would have called him a whore. I love the whore he is. For him, whore means beautiful, means uncalculated, means guiltless and basic—like the angels or the protozoa. When I left L.A. I made him promise to use rubbers. I wanted him to stay healthy. The rubbers won't change things for him; this way he can think he's doing it for me. And he'll like that.

Now I am my Chris for Jack. I am his Chris. Now I understand Chris better. I do love Jack, I just can't be with him all the time. He is different from the others.

The Wild Creatures

He's not furniture, although sometimes our actions make each of us seem so. I'm only as mean as he wants me to be. Chris is the same way with me. It's the way we are. None of us knew exactly what we needed, but we each knew we needed something. That's what we got. I'm not embarrassed about it now. Maybe I know something Scott and Jeff don't know. There's more than one way to get and give affection, and to me, at the right time, they are all acceptable. If Jack and Chris and I are furniture then we are very well-appreciated furniture. We love our periods of use.

One day Chris and I went to the beach. We thought we should try going on an outing together. We didn't have much to talk about. All I could think about was wanting to have sex with him. Later we did. And then we were happy.

Jack came to visit me and brought his new boy-friend. He wanted me to watch him fuck his boyfriend, so I did. Afterward he smiled, and I could tell he was proud for me to see him take the role I usually took in our relationship. His boyfriend loved him and was proud for me to see Jack wanting him. Jack loved his boyfriend and was proud for me to see Jack want him and have him. Then the boyfriend went out for a while and Jack wanted me to fuck him. So I did. And all of this made him happy.

14 Days

I think of the older blonde in the bikini next to me as Mrs. Robinson from *The Graduate.* I imagine the seduction: drinks (vodka) in her hotel room; some '70s, caustically revealing talk on her part ("Why should I get a divorce? To do what?"); '60s nineteen-year-old Dustin Hoffman talk on mine; her tan line as she pulls off the bikini top. Her breasts are unbelievably white next to the tan skin surrounding them. They look like ice. My barely post-adolescent eyes widen in excitement, then quickly attempt to normalize. Her brows wink once, slowly and quietly. She kisses me, places my hands of her breasts, I start to get into it. Then I freak out and run from the room. She sighs and sits on the bed topless, takes another sip of her drink, and inspects her breasts in the mirror. Of course we're actually still in the lounge chairs around the pool. Actually she seems to speak only something other than English, something I wouldn't have been able to understand in the dream. Maybe Dutch. Actually she looks more like Sylvia Miles in *Heat* than Anne Bancroft in *The Graduate.* I wish I looked more like Joe Dalle-sandro in *Heat,* less like Dustin Hoffman.

"How do you like the water?" The man asking me this question is very old, very fat, and wakes me from a sound daze and the Mrs. Robinson dream to ask it. I have my sunglasses on so he can't tell whether I'm awake or asleep (or dead). "How do you like the water here?" I've never seen anyone from around this pool on the adjoining hotel beach, even though the water is warm and the beach private. The sea is a soothing blue green and the white sand so fine it blows off your skin like a light dust when you dry. But no one from this pool goes there. In fact I'm convinced that some of these people don't leave the hotel grounds at all. So I know

The Wild Creatures

immediately that the old man is talking about the pool, not the ocean.

"Fine," I answer, politely, coolly — cool enough I'm hoping to discourage him from continuing.

"You do? Well, I think it's underheated. On the *Golden Odyssey* they check the water temperature every two hours. That's what they should do here. I just can't enjoy a pool if it's not the right temperature. Boy, on the *Golden Odyssey* they really know how to do it right. Ever been on that ship?"

"No." I try to make this sound tired and final. The guy I have my eye on across the pool will never come over. I don't want to encourage this guy to keep talking by informing him that I find the pool water one step below bath temperature already. Any warmer and it would have to be considered a Jacuzzi without the jets. Finally I excuse myself by telling him I'm late for meeting a Brazilian boy on the beach.

A pair of dark arms rises perfectly and beautifully from the blue green water, angling back in, over and over. A solitary swimmer on this stretch of beach. They hypnotize me, those arms. I like it better here than at the pool, but I do like the pool. I like the whole thing more and more: the laziness, the few words, the slow yet continuous pace, checking out the faces and attitudes. It all interests me and when it stops interesting me I still enjoy it. How can I not? Sun, swimming, dreaming.

The dreams that come in this relaxing, balmy heat are sexy, sometimes funny. Odd things from the past come back: swimming lessons at the Y when I was ten. The Beatles on *Ed Sullivan*. A specific *Quick Draw McGraw* cartoon. Going into freezing supermarkets in just the wet swimsuit after lessons. Costume parades on Halloween to the local grocery store in first grade. The first time I saw a guy with a hard-on, in the shower. Odd dreams, the kind you wake up from with a little smile. The actual content drifts away almost immediately. It's

Sam D'Allesandro

the feeling that I sit and savor for a little while, the way I felt in the dream. I shut my eyes and try to recapture it, hoping no one will speak, no one will break it. Not yet. And then it goes and I go for a swim or have a drink or another dream.

It's very hot. During the summer in Rio, the locals say, some people go mad from the sun. Their brains get cooked. You can melt here, starting at your head as it turns to liquid and oozes down the rest of your body the way ice cream does around the cone: progressively more liquid, less body to melt down around.

Most of the Americans and Germans who are the tourists here smear on sun-protection lotion, some skin white to begin with—becomes even whiter. Others use none, stay out all day their first day, turn bright red and then continue to stay out every day. It's painful to look at them. You can practically see the skin cancer setting in. I don't know what happens to these people. Maybe the skin is so dead from the first day that it ends up serving as a protective layer, like wearing clothes. It will, of course, come off when they get home—in big patchy rips and tears. Not at all like the people in the brochure.

There are so many *very* old, not just old, people around this pool that I keep waiting for one to actually die in it. A friend of mine told me that happened when she was at the Managua Hilton. That was before the revolution, long before by several years, as there is no Hilton in Managua now. But it's basically the same: a foreign Hilton or Sheraton or whatever, Managua or Montego Bay or Rio—they're the same. Around the pool the view in the distance (if there is a view) is the only thing that tells you whether you're in California or Miami or 30,000 miles from either. The view from this pool, from this chair, this side of the pool, is of towering cliffs and rock pinnacles that change a hundred colors a hundred times as the sun moves across the afternoon.

The Wild Creatures

Someone's calling out: "Is he still alive?" They're talking about an old man floating on his back in the water. They're joking but everybody looks up for a moment. They do call it the dead man's float. Or is that on your stomach? I'm not sure anyone could actually die that way and keep from sinking. If someone sank to the bottom here, I wonder how long it would take for anyone to notice. There's nothing more unsettling at one of these places than to have the fantasy broken by an ambulance. People *like* the boredom here. It's what they're paying for.

It's no secret that there is a lot of psychological baggage along on these trips that is exactly contrary to a description of what the "idea" is here. The "idea" is the one you get from the brochures, for example. The "idea" is hard to pinpoint but it does *not* include poverty, business, anxiety of any sort, the nonspeaking of English, sunburns, muggings downtown, an incredibly high population of teenage prostitutes, too many Brazilians stuffed into one small city, loud noises, unstoppable hangovers, or running out of money. And it does not include rain. I like it when it rains because it's so easy to go on with whatever you're doing, since it's always a warm rain, usually a gentle rain. It freshens up the air and clears the tourists out of the cafés — they hate it. They worry, I've noticed, about any day that couldn't be called a "tanning day." That's not part of the "idea."

My idea was different anyway. My plane and hotel were free. So I decided to do an experiment — something to do with large American-owned hotels in foreign places. Fourteen days at the Rio Sheraton.

The guy in front of me is trying to teach an Indian man to swim, using an in-the-water lecture format. I picture him retired. He's berating his captured student on his strokes the same way I imagine he used to condescend to his secretary. The same way he condescends now to his wife. His tone with the wife is not my fantasy. I've witnessed it. I'm being unfair, I know. I can't help but see the man as someone needing to teach, to impart his own special knowledge on whatever subject's available wherever he is. I'm sure his wife is glad to have another student around to take her place for a while.

Every day at the pool I hear someone talking about the stock market. I could as easily be at a business lunch. The water, scant swimsuits, uncovered sexual possibilities, and smell of suntan lotion all apparently make no difference when it comes to talking stock. The three guys behind me do it. They're the best-looking at the pool. They're here every day at this time, talking stocks, turning the portable radio up loud (which is not part of the "idea" here), and getting drunk on drinks that come in hollowed-out fruit with little colored parasols sticking out the top. They look gay, seem to cruise, talk straight. I can't define that further—whether I can back up the description's not important, it's how I'm thinking about them, accurate or not. The straight talk keeps me from getting up and trying to meet them.

They're from New Jersey. After a couple days of unintentional eavesdropping I decide guys from New Jersey vacationing in Rio are too sexually ambiguous and confusing for me. Now one's talking about a girl he met in the hotel bar last night. Now one's talking about John Sex, the gay performance artist who strips and masturbates while doing monologues on makeshift stages in New York bars. Now one's talking about passing out before dinner the night before.

As days go by I find there are actually two different sets of these New Jersey guys here. Each group cruises the guys in the other group. They all have carefully Tenaxed hair that doesn't ever enter the pool (let alone the ocean). They lie sweating in lounge chairs until I'm sure one might die of dehydration at any moment. They talk a lot about stocks, nightclubs in New York I know to

The Wild Creatures

be predominantly but not obtrusively gay, and "chicks" (I thought that word was dead but they use it). I'd love to see one of them drop the whole facade, but I'm not necessarily good at making people do that. The Brazilians are more attractive.

The beach along Copacabana is full of the most beautiful boys in the world. Deep brown eyes and perfect bodies. This year the swim fashion is string bikinis so small on the bottom as to require the extensive shaving of the pubic hair for women. All of it, I think. The men don't bother. In terms of serving as a covering these suits are more symbolic than real. People wear them downtown, in restaurants, everywhere. I can't help wondering about the bother of keeping the pubic hair shaved all season, but summer is very important here. And very long.

I met Roberto on the long strip of mosaic sidewalk that starts in front of Ipanema Beach and runs on along Copacabana, all the way to where a rocky point juts out into the bay. The point serves as a cruising area and has the best view in Rio. There are chinning bars for guys to show off on, abandoned buildings, a hundred carefully postured cigarettes glowing in the dark, and sex in rock crevices. The bay laps gently alongside.

When the police came I started the long walk back along Copacabana Beach. The hotels along this stretch are the biggest in Rio. In front of the largest is a one-eighth-mile stretch of sand that is the gay beach, but I didn't find that out until later. Roberto had just finished running the whole length of beach and back—about seven miles I think. Just past dusk. It's too hot to run during the day, he told me. Still the most beautiful chest I'd ever seen was slick and dripping with sweat. That was Roberto's.

Two things happen on our way to the Pappo Gayo Disco. In a shiny, five-day-old imported Italian sports car traveling very fast on a road even shinier with new rain,

41

Sam D'Allesandro

we ram the car in front of us at a stop sign. The car belongs to Roberto's friend. He was driving, is now staring at the little pieces of glass glistening against the blacktop. Although the friend looks on the verge of tears, Roberto tells me not to worry, that accidents are very common here. Everybody has them all the time—it's nothing. A cab takes us the rest of the way to the video bar that's our first stop. That's the second thing. Video is new here. Sitting at multicolored, paint-splattered tables thick with shellac we have a choice of watching over fifty different screens of different sizes and clarity. All show the same image. The audio is loud enough to make talking impossible. I spend the hour staring more at Roberto than at the monitors.

Of course I cheated. The experiment was not to leave the Rio Sheraton and adjoining grounds. After all, from my little hotel balcony, I could see the whole Rio coast-line at night, glittering like a diamond necklace tossed onto the ground in a shape it could only have fallen into once. But I did cheat. I walked the entire stretch of Ipanema and Copacabana every evening. I did meet Roberto. I did go to Pappo Gayo—the disco with the same name as a Brazilian cocoa drink. I did go to the *supermarcado* in a rainstorm, to Fiorucci's, and up to Corcovado, the famous Christ statue on the mountain. And I went to the cemetery.

The cemetery is full of cats, plastic flowers, and pictures of the dead leaning in gilt frames against crumbling and ornate Christs. Christs, Marys, and crosses—all cheap plaster slowly melting with each new rain. Those who live here often leave letters for the dead. You can see the little envelopes with the name written formally across the front, gripped by a masonry hand or held between stems in a bunch of roses. Roberto and I kissed here for the first time.

It's been six weeks. In the morning I kiss him all over to

The Wild Creatures

wake him. One thousand kisses. He wants us to stay in bed together all day. Again. The apartment's in Copacabana, close to the beach. From the balcony on the sixth floor I can see Sugarloaf. I have to remind myself now that that's a view that's famous. It's in all the brochures. I only vaguely remember those now. This morning I watch Roberto shave while I have my coffee. It's not that I'm so romantic; I just can't get over seeing his perfect arms in motion. The coffee's Brazilian.

He takes pictures of me as I'm stepping out of the shower naked. I don't care. So far he hasn't been able to find anything to do that would annoy me. I teach him about safe sex. He gets me to wear a Speedo bathing suit downtown that's skimpier than the smallest pair of men's underwear I've ever seen. They're used to seeing a lot of skin here but for me it's like waking up naked in high school. It's comfortable once I get over being uncomfortable doing it.

By the time I realize that all the boys in Rio want him it's too late for paranoia. I already know that the one Roberto wants is me. Why, I don't know, but I know. I don't ask if he likes being with me so much because he doesn't have any design jobs at the moment. I don't ask whether he really thinks I'm beautiful when he says so, or if he says that to all the foreign boys. It really doesn't matter. I do wonder whether he's sensually insatiable because he's Brazilian, or if it's the other way around. He looks like a younger, more-handsome, better-built, very-tan Martin Sheen. When I was still at the hotel and would think about him, I'd get what felt like an amazed look on my face, shake my head slowly back and forth, and murmur "God" — meaning God, he's so good-looking I can't believe it. Everybody's that way for somebody but some people are that way for almost everybody.

There are still things I want to see in Rio, and Roberto surprises me by being willing to go almost anywhere, to places he's been before a hundred times. But he won't go to the Disco Rio on Sunday afternoons. And after the second time, he would not go back to the cemetery with me to take more photographs. I skip the disco and we watch an old Bergman movie on TV in dubbed French with Portuguese subtitles. A girl walks through a dream where all the people in her life are mannequins. I think to myself: *That was me before*. Now there's Roberto. I'm sure he's real...or else a very real dream.

Teddy Kennedy

Teddy Kennedy is fat now. He sweats a lot, and he isn't sexy like Bobby. His wife went crazy. All she eats is alcohol and Valium. One of his kids has only one leg.

Teddy Kennedy wears awful suits, and those glasses that look like they've been cut in half, which I don't like. After all, they look silly enough on Cyrus Vance, and everything looks worse on Teddy.

Teddy Kennedy has a very hairy chest. I like hairy chests but I would not sleep with Teddy Kennedy. Marilyn slept with John—I would have slept with Bobby—but never, never with Teddy.

Teddy Kennedy has a poor driving record. I don't know what his insurance is like, but I'm sure he can pay it. Kennedys have lots of money. Teddy's nephew uses it to buy heroin. He gets it in Harlem, then drives back to New England to shoot up on a sailboat. And I've heard his grandfather was a smuggler.

Teddy Kennedy has his face on *Newsweek* this week. I have a subscription. I looked real good. I don't think I can stand to see his face as much as you have to when a guy's president. I doubt if anyone would take the time to shoot him in the head. They'll just keep shooting his picture instead.

He's not very attractive. I'm voting for Jerry Brown because he's gay and sexy.

A Fine Feat Hered Friend
with Kevin Killian

San Francisco propaganda sells Lombard Street as the "crookedest street in the world," but the stretch of Lombard with all the motels on it is straight, flat, and suburban. Across the boulevard sits an ancient IHOP, blue and orange and clunky. I directed my friend to this part of town when he came to San Francisco on a visit. He isn't really a friend, he's a friend of a friend, and I never laid eyes on him until he came to us from Washington, DC. "You wanted reasonable," I tell him. "This is reasonable." In the motel room the air-conditioning isn't great—not broken, exactly—but it stutters in our ears. Sometimes on and sometimes off, even though we bang it with the heels of our hands to put it on an even keel. The two of us lie on one chenille-covered twin bed, heads propped up on pillows, watching the traffic pull up and away from the parking lot. His room's on the first floor because he's afraid of heights. He had insisted, over the phone, on securing a first-floor room, his voice strangely attenuated, like the flame of a candle, flickering.

His name is Andy. Maybe his name is Andy.

In the kitchenette some honeymooners had left an opened bottle of flat champagne, an omen or talisman of I don't know what. Nothing very good. It doesn't say much for housekeeping if they could have missed this big bottle, a magnum. The friend of my friend points this out, but as I remind him, he wanted something reasonable, and reasonable includes a little dirt. We're not tidy Felix Ungers here in San Francisco, we're authentic.

"Okay," Andy says. "The city always looked so pretty in the postcards and in *Flower Drum Song*."

46

The Wild Creatures

"And *Bullitt* and *Vertigo*," I add. He seems to perk up at this, and we continue to list the many movies filmed in SF, him adding a bunch I've never heard of, so many in fact I begin to think, he's really made a study of this. Thereafter he intrigues me, because people with a passion have something going for them, don't you think, even if it's a propensity for what my mother used to call *no good*. And he's got the dark eyes and pale, pale skin of a Matt Dillon type, a bit older and beefier. He seems truthful on the face of it, but—but what? Inside my head I find myself thinking, kvetching really, *But I wouldn't come to San Francisco if I was afraid of heights, has he seen* Vertigo *or does he just like to talk about it like every other movie queen?* Did you know that the famous von Stroheim masterpiece *Greed* was filmed in San Francisco in 1923? Again, I can't tell if Andy had seen it or just liked to boast of his wealth of trivia knowledge. Later it turns out that Andy isn't afraid of heights so much as of fires and not being able to escape burning to death, should the city burn down again as it had in *San Francisco* and *The Towering Inferno*. And that's why he'd asked me to get him a first-floor room.

Lying next to him on the bed, I start to feel the way you do when you're stretched out nearby someone new. The sun from the window slants in across his face and up his nostrils and all across his cheekbones. Maybe we are supposed to start fooling around a little. It is that kind of day.

But inaction gets in the way; I feel more reserved than usual. Instead, lying on the bed, we watch as a couple gets out of their car and looks around, stretching in the parking lot. Working out the kinks by bending from the waist. Obviously tourists, with loud Hawaiian shirts and binoculars saddled around their necks. From the back seat of the car issue two young boys, nine or ten. They just stand on the curb, hitting each other drowsily, as though they've had a long ride from Montana or

Sam D'Allesandro

wherever, and can't work up enough intensity really to give each other any good whacks. I have my own fear, of being bored to death, a fear so intense it curdles my mind and I can't concentrate on the wisecracks Andy's making about tourists. Then it goes away and I'm feeling a little panicky, thinking, *I don't know much about this guy and here I am practically in bed with him*. Correction, we're in bed, just on the covers though, if that's any consolation. Not like I haven't had sex on top of covers. He's a lawyer. At least that's what my DC friend told me. I didn't ask to see his diploma. He says he has a shot at being a congressman someday.

"Not too many gay congressmen, are there?"

"Life is made up of compartments," he assures me. "And nobody in my political life is ever going to know about my sex life."

"Oh, don't people just *know*," I reply, feeling argumentative. "Everybody's got gaydar, even the Senate."

"Don't I look straight to you?"

To tell you the truth, no guy looks real straight to me when his lips are only a few inches from mine and they're parted, trembling, white teeth, red tongue showing through and he's reeking of some kind of alluring chemical smell.

"Sure you do," I say. I put my fingertip to his lips, traced the curved contours. Lying down, his straight edge was starting to decompress, like one of those life preservers that slip around your neck as your plane goes down. Then I told him my Hardy Boys story.

When I was young the first books I read were the Hardy Boys books my older brother left lying around the house. *The Tower Treasure, The House on the Cliff, What Happened at Midnight*. Sexy titles. Everybody knows about the Hardy Boys, but many forget they had a chubby friend, Chet Morton, whose sister, Iola, was a local girl Frank or Joe used to date. From the very earliest time I can remember I thought Chet was a fag. A gang

The Wild Creatures

had captured one of the Hardy Boys, and it stuck with me, a truly terrifying scene, he was bound up in ropes and for some reason Chet Morton's loyalty is momentarily implicated. Maybe he introduced the Hardys to this gang (for he's stupid as well as fat). Frank or Joe is all tied up with serious rope, so is Chet, and the gang has left them in this attic and has set fire to it. I remember Frank spits on the fire trying to put it out.

"Like Gulliver pissing on the fire among the Lilliputians," Andy says. I forgot he was afraid of fire, or maybe his fear brought this other train of thought right to the forefront of my mind.

"Anyhow Frank says to Chet, 'A fine feathered friend you turned out to be,' but there was a misprint, or typo, in the book, and the word 'feathered,' which was all the way on the right-hand margin, broke in two, but the compositor failed to insert the hyphen, so it read, 'A fine feat hered friend you turned out to be.' And I was baffled. I literally failed to recognize the word 'feathered.' I drew a complete blank. Like that sky there. Nothing in it. Not that I would have known what a 'fine feathered friend' means, nor do I now, but 'feat' and 'hered' seemed like two such odd words to link together, it baffled me and it scared me. Maybe it was the word, or quasi-word, 'hered.'"

"Makes Chet sound *gendered.*"

"Like he was a 'her.'"

"And everybody knew," Andy says with a long sigh. Then he gets up off the bed and pulls the curtains down and the room, in the sunny parking-lot heat, goes dark and cool. "Everybody knew all about Chet Morton and everyone will know all about me."

"Well, nobody knows 'all about' anyone," I reply.

Andy slumps back into the bed next to me and fiddles with his drink, a lonely little glass sitting on the glass-topped table by the big ironwork lamp.

"So you think those boys are gay?"

49

Sam D'Allesandro

"What boys?"

"Those two boys who got out of the Chevy with their parents."

"They kind of reminded me of me and my brother," I recall. Maybe it was the way they were hitting each other.

If we concentrate hard we can still hear the two boys hitting each other with rolled up copies of magazines and road maps, lazily swatting each other like mosquitoes. Mom and Dad are out of earshot so they're calling each other vulgar kid names like "dickwad."

"One of them's gay, the other isn't."

"The older one is."

I catch Andy's eye. *The "older one" is still pretty young*, I'm thinking, *maybe Mr. Future Congressman's attuned to the sex appeal of young boys*. But in that case you'd think he'd be vacationing in Thailand or Sri Lanka, not San Francisco. You wouldn't think he'd be rolling over in bed toward me still in his suit, his tie flapping onto the bedspread with that look that says, well here we are, what about it.

"Are we here just to talk about the Hardy Boys or are we here to—?" His hand isn't quite a fist yet; I see his palm rubbing his crotch through the suit material. I learned early on how to tell when a man's excited, and this one is getting there pretty damn quick.

I don't like the way he's so closeted, but I wind up with a big grin on my face.

"I like your suit. When I saw you come out of the taxicab you looked so damn elegant it gave me a hard-on. Quite a heady one of course."

"Anyone can see those boys had to grow up to be fags. At least I think so."

He puts his hand on mine. Oh glory, oh joy. Beatific horniness overflows, cascading lightly over the rim to softly touch down. We like each other enough to ignore the things we don't like. Even in ourselves. We are earth-

50

The Wild Creatures

bound for now, after all. Finally he moves his gaze to mine and I reach around and slither my hand under his belt.

I like a man's ass best when he's been sitting on it all day. When it's sat in his office chair or been crammed into an uncomfortable plane seat traveling thousands of miles to come see me. When, lying on his stomach on the hotel bed, it manages over the course of a few hours to inflate, to grow steadily under my hand. When the damp silk of his boxers clings to it and I catch my breath, watch it come back to life. Like a heat-and-serve roll. No gym bunnies for me, I want office workers, shows they have a brain not just a butt. His ass, moist through the silk, a little funky, it's alive. I crane my neck, lower my jaw, bite a little bit through the silk. "I just eat this underwear shit up," he says, if I understand him correctly.

"They didn't have this part in *Flower Drum Song*," I remind him. But he is too far gone to hear me.

One of the boys outside throws his brother's little knapsack into the pool. "Douchebag," cries the victim. All of a sudden Andy snaps back to attention. He's *really present* as we say in California. You can hear these family noises out there somewhere, and you can be nose-deep inside a magnificently round butt, congressional meat, and somehow the nuclear family comes in, breaks in, impinges and, well, I have to say it, bites you in the ass... I'm all like, Joan Didion's flat out wrong, it should be we *rim in order to live....*

Jimmy

He was new in town and didn't know where to go. I met him at the cigarette store and we just started talking. He talked to me more than most of my friends do. So I even told him my real name. I took him to the park to see the ducks.

Later on the street he said he had a good time. It started raining and we both went home. That night I saw him at the disco I'd told him about. He looked all right, sharp like me. He was wearing a black sweater and smoking his new cigarettes.

I asked him to come home with me. He thought about it for a minute and then he said okay. I remember he liked the Mustang. When we got to my place I sat him on the bed, and he ran his hand slowly over the spread. I got him a glass of water and watched him drink.

When he got toward the end I couldn't see his mouth or nose through the up-tipped glass. I fell in love with his drinking brown eyes. The phone rang and when I came back he was gone. He left one contact lens on my dresser. His roommate told me he went back to Grand Rapids. I think about him all the time.

All I Want Is to Die Famous

Naked in the blinding machine at Today's Tan, doing my best to get a good burn before Rio, I can't help thinking — like always — this time about Carol Wayne drowning in Acapulco. Carol Wayne: actress, gameshow celebrity, Hollywood resident. I read in the obituary that she'd done the Carson show over two hundred times. She couldn't even swim they say, so why was she out in the water all alone? That's what I'd like to know. I wonder if she was as burned at the time as I'm becoming now in this nuclear coffin at Today's Tan. Maybe she just had to cool off, swim or not. On the way out they hand me a flyer, "Coming Soon: No Limits, No Liabilities, No Reasons, Just What Everybody Needs in TODAY'S WORLD." "TODAY'S WORLD" as opposed to yesterday's I guess or as opposed to tomorrow's world. I didn't quite get it. I figure the present is passing on to innovation so quickly anyway, why bother with it? That's what I think. Maybe that's what Carol Wayne was thinking.

Question: how many *Wheel of Fortune*s, how many *$20,000,000 Pyramid*s, how many *Johnny Carson* appearances does a girl have to do before she's a star? She found the answer scribbled in black lipstick on the back of a bleached peroxide bottle on a filthy beach in Acapulco, following the pert and perky tilt and bob of the plastic container back out on the waves to a death sea. Scene: ambulance, crowd, attendants, body, all under an azure sky. A remarkable quality of light here. Motion: the ambulance begins to move up and down in a rhythm, push, lift, push, lift, as the young attendant tries to press life back into the siliconed chest. Is this getting too down? This is what Hollywood dreams are made of. Ask anyone.

In an out-of-the-way restaurant in downtown L.A.,

Sam D'Allesandro

not far from West Hollywood, poured-cement tables, poured-cement walls, poured-cement floors, pink lighting and a jagged fish tank, the drinks expensive and the location dangerous. I came in here to soak up some atmosphere, and immediately I'm annoyed, wishing there was a television set or someone drunk enough to entertain or something. Ambience alone is not enough to drain my tension. There are times when reality is best ignored; I know that, I'm no dummy, I have learned from the mistakes of others. Life is no bowl of cherries, especially here in Glamorville. Witness: Mary Hartman, cancellation her only reward for coping with every creeping crisis known to the suburban dweller; Jo Ann Castle, fired after thirty years on *Lawrence Welk* (contract no good no more); the Monkees' screaming slide from top of the '60s throwaway culture heap to the slimy pit of media burnout (two short years in the making); Frank Gifford, actor, athlete, stud, laughing all the way to the bank, castrated amidst a nightmare of chocolate brown and toilet-bowl white Frigidaire refrigerators (all recorded on videotape); Carol Wayne found dead on the beach in a glitzy Mexico resort town.

She said: I'm gonna make it in this town if it kills me. My name's gonna be in that goddamn cement in front of that stupid theater if I have to pour the shit myself. Listen, there's more than one way to get ahead in this business, and I'm going to try them all. Tell me who to fuck and I will fuck, fuck you, fuck the public, let them cram *me* down their throats for a while. All I want is to die famous — there's nothing else to do as far as I can tell.

At Venice Beach it's a party of new dolphin-stretch Speedos, suntan oil, and bikini combs. These boys won't even go near the water, let alone the girls. There's a retarded man in white jockey underwear that he keeps bunching up around his waist so that his balls hang out. He's talking to us, but we don't know what he's saying. We feel sorry for him, but we wish he'd go away — no,

The Wild Creatures

he's not with us, everyone, announcement: we don't
know him, we don't usually even come to this beach,
we're not even from here. There's no stronger reality
amidst these piles of constructed bodies than a retarded
man with his balls exposed. This is HOLLYWOOD. This is
where Carol Wayne became a star, lived, dieted, did the
Wheel of Fortune, met Johnny Carson, took off for
Acapulco. This is where she'll be buried and remembered even after the *$20,000,000,000 Pyramid* has hit
network bankruptcy. We loved her live, now we love her
dead. Here it's all the same, only better.

Jane and Sam

At first Jane and I were repelled by our attraction to each other. We were afraid of it. We didn't know what it meant. Then she taught me how to french-kiss. After that we never regained any of the control we might have had earlier. We snuck out to smoke a joint and ended up in a graveyard. It was snowing, everything looked white and clean. Her wild hair made a cave around our faces. First she made me keep my tongue still while hers moved inside of my mouth and explored. I felt like a little baby being touched, doing nothing while she took care of me. She smelled good. I could hear the snow falling, little puff noises. We slowly worked up to both using our tongues at the same time. She laughed a little at the way I kissed with my eyes open. I didn't care. I wanted to see, to watch her. I couldn't name the qualities my hands were finding. Warm skin, the soft body, hair damp and cool with snow on the outside layer, warm and dry beneath—no matter how much I touched her she still felt strange and indefinable.

After the kissing lesson we rolled around in a bank of snow making angel shapes with our arms and legs. When we stood up for a look, some of the angels looked more like monsters. Angels turned into monsters. I guess we needed to mess things up a little. Our sex organs worked now but we were still children. We were adults. We were afraid of the adults we were becoming and we didn't want to be children anymore. She was the one who wanted to have sex first; I was afraid. When we took drugs I was always the one who wanted to do it first; she was afraid. We both did the things we were afraid of as long as the other knew we were afraid and still wanted to do it.

Half of everything: half-grown, half-child, half-

The Wild Creatures

woman, half-man. Is that adolescence? We thought adolescence was for junior varsity basketball players and the pep squad and horny, pimple-faced jerks — all pumped up about Teen Center dances and homecoming games. For Jane and me, it was dark places. Abandoned buildings and hiding spots for sex and dangerous tests of loyalty. On mescaline we raced trains to the crossing in a beat-up old truck, trying to get across the tracks before the smashup. Jane loved the rush of the big engine lights coming at her. She'd start ricocheting around the cab of the truck like a pinball, like Faye Dunaway in her death scene in *Bonnie and Clyde,* screaming and laughing and grabbing onto me or her head or the dash. She wanted the whole truck to shake as much as she was. I was more intent, trying to make sure we won the race. Later a friend's mother was killed when her car stalled on the same tracks. She could've gotten away but she had two neighbor kids with her and got hit trying to throw them free. We wouldn't have had a good reason like that if we'd gotten hit. It's just that there was nothing else to do. Our town was so damned small. We were unsatisfied more than adolescent. Of adolescence we were each robbed, spared, not involved. It was a different storm for us. Things were out of our control.

Much later, in New York, older, still too young to get into bars, Randy and I usually ended up watching late-night television. First *Mary Hartman, Mary Hartman,* then *Metro News, The George Burns and Gracie Allen Show,* and finally the late movie. It always turned out to be a Ma and Pa Kettle feature. *Ma and Pa Kettle, Ma and Pa Kettle in Waikiki, Ma and Pa Kettle Go to Hollywood,* Ma and Pa Kettle Happy All Day. Nothing ever really bothered them. They had twelve kids they named after the months of the year. Sometimes *Ma and Pa Kettle in Waikiki* would show for five nights in a row. We developed something of a quasi-religious relationship with Ma and Pa. And with Mary Hartman. Ma and Pa gave me an example of adaptability in any situation. It was Mary Hartman who taught me the key to problem-solving. No matter who came into Mary's kitchen, no matter how awful the problem, Mary always had the answer. Have a cup of coffee. "Have a cup of coffee," I said finally to Hugo. It did seem to calm him down a little. He kept repeating, "Jane changed. Right. *Scheiße*."

This is the same Jane. My Jane. Now she and Hugo are lovers. Or at least they were. I'm not sure Jane would consider it love exactly, but she's not too concerned with love as a question anyway. They're both practical in their own way. It's practical for Jane, it seems to Jane, not to worry about love and happiness and to just live in a way that's somewhat comfortable. For her that means keeping the definitions of a relationship a little vague. Parameters flexible. It is practical for Hugo, it seems to Hugo, to consider Jane and himself as much more of a traditional couple than Jane would, and to therefore feel he's taken care of the love/sex/relationship questions. It's important for him to be able to consider questions as either active or completed. Very clean and efficient. An effective use of time here. That's important to Hugo. Everything worked fine this way until the occasion when Hugo asked Jane if she loved him, expecting a standard but gratifying (for Hugo) "Of course I do, don't be silly" reply. Instead she responded with a stammer that led into an "I'm not sure love even exists" stance. Then Hugo doubted whether he had taken care of all the love/sex/relationship questions after all. Not so efficient and effective after all. Jane and Hugo are no Ma and Pa Kettle in the adaptability department. Think of Ma and Pa Kettle at an impasse.

Hugo comes to me because he thinks I know Jane better than he does. He's right about that. I said, "Listen, Hugo, you can't expect to solve all your problems in one morning around the kitchen table." I was thinking that he probably can't expect to solve all of his problems,

The Wild Creatures

period. I was thinking how Jane and I are not anything like Jane and Hugo. We never were.

Here's how it was: Jane unpredictable. She moody and I moodier. Both untrustworthy, both aware of that, neither expecting the other not to be. We weren't Victorians, we didn't expect monogamy. Bringing two difficult people together was bound to, at times, be violent. We knew that. We needed to throw our dice together for a while. Jane thought I might be gay, she said she could feel it in me, could recognize some of the same targets—that's the sort of wacky symbiosis we were dealing with. One of us was always bleeding into the other. If it happened too much, one of us would get angry and pull away. It was too painful to see our own needs in the other all the time. We both always came back. Affairs were only something to run away to when we got scared.

Eventually we stopped fighting each other, and started realizing how complete we were together. We had an unspoken pact, like the lovers in *Hiroshima Mon Amour*. A synchronicity was developing. Sometimes we were man and woman, sometimes I became a woman and we were lesbians, sometimes she became a man and we were homosexuals. We were always changing, but the ways we changed always still seemed to work. Maybe we were duplicates—each helping the other thrash a temporary identity out of the miasma we'd been born into. Neither of us seemed to fit in anywhere except with each other. Neither of us fit in, but we needed each other to find out how we didn't. After a while nothing could throw us off the track of each other.

I can tell Hugo's not getting my drift. To his thinking, you have a problem and a solution. Just eliminate the possibilities until you hit on the right one. He says Jane's changed. She's not the same as when he met her. She's different now. He tells me that it's not so much the way

59

Jane's changed that's bothering him, it's the very fact that she has. He can't count on her to stay constant. He doesn't know how to react to her now that he's not sure what her response might be. They learned how to get along together once; they cannot keep relearning to do that. That's the way Hugo sees it. Jane will not see it that way, I know. Think of Ma and Pa Kettle with irreconcilable differences. Think of Ma and Pa Kettle on a bummer.

Hugo's right in thinking that I know Jane better than he does, but in the end I don't have any good advice for him. Nothing I say about a relationship not being a finished product seems to make any difference. I don't want to make a flaky American out of Hugo, or teach him a lot of vague '70s jargon for relationships, but it does bother me a little that he thinks like my grandfather. I decide to fix him another cup of coffee.

Sometimes it's not easy to adapt when someone changes. Sometimes the change may require a retreat, or even abandonment. Sometimes. That's what Hugo is afraid he might have to do, abandon or be abandoned. That may be what Jane has already done. I get a note from her the next day on my car windshield: "Leaving this afternoon for Mexico City, couldn't get you on the phone, don't tell Hugo. Back in a couple of days—Jane."

Ma Kettle sits in a booth at the Waikiki Hilton writing a postcard to Pa. Through the window she can see people sunbathing around the ice-blue pool. For a moment someone looks up at the window. Ma smiles, gives a little wave before realizing that people can't actually see in through the tinted glass, goes back to the postcard—"Pa: I guess we both know something's wrong, had to get away, having a wonderful time—Ma."

Jane walks into my kitchen with a six-pack of beer under her arm. "How was Mexico?" "I sunburned my tits in Acapulco. Let's get drunk—Hugo's driving me out of

60

The Wild Creatures

my mind." While she's in the shower I make pesto. She likes that. I don't often pamper her. She doesn't need pampering very often, but I figure if she's depressed and has sunburned tits maybe I'd better try to improve the evening's odds. She'll stay over tonight. She might be moving in until she finds a new place. I don't know yet; she knows she can. She likes Neil, who lives with me and is in Florida. Neil's not here right now but he's important. The three of us get along well. Hugo never could keep up with the banter when we all got together. I always felt bad about that, but I never knew what to do to make it easier for him. I finally decided that it would never be easy for him and accepted his discomfort. We liked Hugo. It just never quite worked right.

I guess something worked for Jane and Hugo when they were alone. For a while. Whatever it was isn't working much now. I wonder if that could happen to Neil and me. We're different from Jane and Hugo. What's happening to them wouldn't happen to us, but something different with the same result could. After all, things change. I imagine myself as a better survivor than Hugo. I imagine Neil as easier to part amiably with than Jane would be.

We smoke a joint after dinner, something Jane is more prone to do than I am these days. She likes smoking together. Why do people have to make easy things so difficult? — she wants to know. I don't answer. She isn't really looking for me to; she knows we'd both like the answer to that question.

After the joint I do the dishes. I like the way the warm soapy water feels sliding against the plates. Jane puts on a Laura Nyro record. She likes to put on Laura Nyro when she's feeling depressed. It helps her to enjoy the depression more. This time she tricks herself. "Up on the Roof" comes on and she accidentally slips into a good mood. She dances into the kitchen, swaying, smiling, singing along ("When this old world starts

Sam D'Allesandro

getting me down...") and takes my hands from the sink and puts them around her waist. I'm smiling too. I'm thinking how easy it is for us to be together. Neil would be annoyed at my soapy hands soaking through his shirt the way they're soaking through Jane's robe. Her skin shows through, it seems covered with only a thin layer of tissue, not really covered at all. We sway past the stove and into the living room. Not putting too much effort into the dancing. We don't care if we're awkward or miss a beat. Hugo would care, would have to dance correctly or not dance at all. Jane would have laughed at him and tried to loosen him up. Jane's tired of trying to loosen Hugo up. So she's dancing with me.

Jane's written Hugo off, I can tell. It's over, finished, "on the rocks" she'll tell me the next day. Probably at breakfast over coffee. By lunchtime she'll be breaking the news to Hugo. By midafternoon he'll be in my kitchen and I'll be pouring him a cup of coffee, feeling none too helpful, and finding the Mary Hartman technique perhaps not so effective after all.

Jane will be the one who says, "It's just not going to work." Hugo will probably agree. He'll still feel lousy. So will Jane, lousy and a little guilty. She is not casual about her relationships these days. I think the abrupt ending of this one appears more casual than she would like. She says that Jane and Hugo is a relationship that never should have been in the first place. Hugo (she starts, loudly) was stubborn, inflexible, incompatible, kind of sexy (softer), incredibly sweet at times...wrong, a mistake (steady). Now come tears. Jane is not as tough as she likes to think. Sometimes it's not as easy to do what we do as it may seem to someone watching us do it. Ma Kettle sits in the Aloha Lounge sipping a Mai Tai and thinking about Pa.

At some point since my kissing lesson in the graveyard things changed for Jane and me. It's not so important to

62

The Wild Creatures

know everything that led up to that point. Basically we needed to find out what it was like to be without each other. Jane went off to South America for two months and stayed for a year and a half. I moved to New York and started watching late-night television. The change came almost that simply. Here's how it went when Jane came back: I introduced her to Randy, she laughed, calmly looked into his eyes, asked if he would mind if she and I slept together that night. Randy didn't mind. Jane was shocked by his cool. She liked him right off. The next night Jane and Randy and I slept together. Randy loved to watch Jane and me kiss. He said he felt like he was watching me kiss myself. He liked the narcissism of it. Jane got into sucking Randy's cock while he and I kissed. Randy got into Jane's breasts. He'd never slept with a woman before. Her nipples intrigued him. He was afraid of her vagina.

Sometimes when the three of us were in bed together I didn't know which parts of me were touching Jane and which parts were touching Randy, whether it was Randy sucking my cock or Jane. Together they felt so familiar, comfortable yet indefinable. Sometimes I needed to sleep just with Randy, sometimes just with Jane. Sometimes it didn't matter. That combination went on for quite a while.

Now when Jane and I sleep together we sleep very close, like spoons. Like dozing kittens. It's different than when we were teenagers or when we were with Randy. Now we don't want sex from each other as much as we want to be close to each other. To warm and calm each other. We used to use sex as a means of getting that. Now we don't need to. Now for me, sex means Neil. For Jane it was Hugo, will be someone else. What Jane and I get from each other is different, quiet, steady. We're so used to each other.

At night our breathing synchronizes into a nice, tranquilizing purr. I wake up and listen. The monotony

63

Sam D'Allesandro

of the sound relaxes me. We usually end up with a light blanket over us at most, even in winter the bundle of our bodies produces that much heat. If we add Neil to the tangle even a sheet may be too much, but Jane and I mostly sleep together when Neil's away. Jane likes both Neil and Randy. She thinks I should have kept them both. That way we could all live and sleep together in one giant king-size bed. For me it's just too different of a feeling (the feeling of sleeping with Neil and that of sleeping with Jane) to sleep with them together too often. Of course if Jane's feeling lonely she climbs in with us. She always takes the middle.

Jane comes into the bedroom with a glass of water. I recognize the smell of her just-shampooed hair, still wet from the shower. She asks about Neil. Neil's okay. Neil and I are okay. I think what's happening with her and Hugo made Jane worry about Neil and me for a moment. Neil's important, he's just not here right now. He's entertained by Jane. Now we'll have a third person to play Trivial Pursuit with. Now we'll have someone else to inspire us to go out to new places. There's no problem here. It's not that I'm any better at finding adaptable lovers than Jane is. I just happened to get Neil and she got Hugo. Probably either of us could last well and long in a relationship with Neil. If he were straight maybe Jane would be the lover and I'd be the other-and-also person.

In the bathroom I notice evidence that Jane's returned. I see her brush on the counter and the dental floss moved from a neglected spot in the cabinet to the windowsill by the sink. Her contact lens case is right next to mine, and in the spot where Neil's will be when he gets back. If I think about it, I could come up with quite a few ways in which we seem to amuse each other that when someone else is doing the same thing would be annoying. A lot of things the three of us have in com-

64

The Wild Creatures

mon. We all like reading a trashy novel after reading one that's complicated. We all like a good argument and obvious sarcasm. We all like Jane's lasagna, Laura Nyro (still), Mickey Rourke's acting and Robert Altman's movies. We each enjoy some sort of weird humor in the *National Enquirer,* Liz Smith's column (actually Neil hates Liz Smith but he enjoys hating her), and *Entertainment Tonight.* We don't expect things to be perfect. So far getting along's enough.

Before I come to bed I refill the glass of water Jane got earlier and put it on the floor on her side. I've always done that; she wakes up thirsty, I know. She groans in her sleep. Jane groans and I talk. Then usually in the middle of the night I wake up thirsty and reach over the top of her to get the glass.

Speedboys

When I was twelve we rode banana bikes (the kind with phallic seats low to the ground) all over town, and I learned to do wheelies across a desert of pavement when the playground was empty on weekends. Riding proud and strong in this pack, we were young urban wolves, as free, fast, and independent as our wheels and feet could make us, all over the little town that couldn't hold us still.

High in the big tree in Vance's backyard, we were invisible to all but each other. Long afternoons were spent watching the sky and the big field in back of the school, beyond the fence we'd have to climb over to make our midnight raids on nights when we slept in the tent. Scaling up and over the cyclone-mesh barrier, daring the jump from the top to the ground, being careful to miss the rim of barbed wire—we'd run through the field as if our bodies never needed to slow down, our bursting lungs having no right to force a stop to our expedition for rest; moving on, faster, moving on, faster...

We crouched flat to the ground to avoid Tommy Smith's light, praying the grass would provide cover as his patrol car scanned the territory, wondering for a split second how we could have dared trespassing and what would happen to us now that we were about to be caught—then up and moving and laughing, having evaded the light once more, with no recollection of second thoughts a moment earlier.

Retrieving cigarettes from a pipe in the ground, off and onward until some dark and hidden place would beckon us to stop and enter, we'd huddle and smoke, smug and satisfied in our recklessness. Warm in the safety of an unlit corner, the dark and deserted was ours

The Wild Creatures

to possess for the moment, silent witness to our jokes and gossip, and the sound of our voices going lower as the night grew later, the talk more serious...

This is the talk that had taken the whole night to get to. Talk of fears and anticipation: what to do when it's time to be drafted; when each new hurdle comes, as we know they will, as we have seen them come to our older brothers; wondering who will be the one who just can't make it. Is it me? "Well, I'm a hell of a lot smarter than Rick and Mike. Those guys have a lot more to worry about than I do."

And the moment of vulnerability passes as anxiety is pushed into boastful laughter, or sometimes reassurances from best friends when it's time to love each other without letting anyone know that's what you're doing. Dealing fast with fear of the too-serious, speedboys race to meet an untried world before the hot fix of young blood pales and the night begins to show its cold.

My Day with Judy

"If it's really gray out, there's nothing you can do to wake up." That was Judy's observation. Ocean Beach certainly was gray. As if we'd entered a black-and-white movie somewhere along the line. The sand and sky and water all looked like variations on the same monochromatic scale. And of course we were wearing black. And Buster, the dog Buster, is black and white like always. He runs ahead of us, sniffing at shells and scratching up a little sand here and there; Buster loves to catch the Frisbee when Judy throws it. According to Judy, he pretends it's a flying saucer, like the ones he's seen in old '50s movies on TV (smart dog). Occasionally he makes a barking, hysterical run at the retreating waves. That never lasts too long. There's no fear of Buster running into the water without return. He seems to be motorized by some sort of leftover primal hunting energy that he no longer knows what to do with. That's city life. Not much hunting in the Mission for a boxer like Buster. He has another purpose—protecting Judy. It's not so much the idea that Buster would attack someone that tried to harm her, it's more the hope that no one would be willing to with something as funny-looking as Buster standing by. Judy takes him whenever she goes, even to work at the car parts warehouse. It's like Buster works there too. Everyone knows him.

Judy expects the worst at all times and tries to prepare for it. Before she got Buster, she carried a knife. Now Buster's jagged spiked collar has taken the knife's place, as if Judy could whip it off and bludgeon someone to death with the little one-inch spikes if need be. It's all a matter of psychology. For instance, Judy feels safer walking with me than alone or with one of her girlfriends, even though I carry little of the preparedness

68

The Wild Creatures

and none of the weaponry that she and most of her girlfriends have incorporated. I would feel safer walking with Judy than alone or with most of my other friends or with my girlfriend (if I had one). I figure Judy's attitude and sneer alone should be enough to neutralize any would-be assailant.

Here's what she's telling me now: "That's why they call this the suicide belt—it's overcast ninety percent of the year. Suicide statistics around Ocean Beach are through the roof. I read an article about it. [*Pause.*] I kind of like the gray. Sometimes it's nice for a change. Easy on the senses."

Judy's a big fan of the New Technology Center's mass destruction events: crashing cars; fighting robots covered in dead animal corpses; lots of noise, smoke, breaking glass. One time they had an enormous machine, like a dinosaur, that sucked up iron balls from a pile on the ground, relayed them upward through a series of levers in the metal neck, and then hurled them out through the mouth at sheets of glass. That's all it did. Ball after ball, sheet after sheet. Judy said she liked the pointlessness of that one. I like the robotized animal corpses myself. They terrify me. It's weird to imagine those guys picking up crummy, rotten, maggoty animal corpses off the highways and then molding them around the little machines so they can move again. They find mostly dogs, raccoons, an occasional coyote, or maybe an extra-enormous cat. What the corpse was doesn't matter as much as what it will become. These gruesome machine resurrections were once as frisky and cute as Buster is now. They always hit me as both kind of sweet and a little evil. "The thing is," Judy points out, "those guys don't care about sweet and evil anyway; they just want to see if it can be done. You know, inanimate things made animate."

Being part of the New Technology Center's audience can be hazardous; grease or sparks or shrapnel always flying around, ripping up our clothes—hard on the senses is actually our norm. I guess appreciating one extreme can make the opposite seem like a sort of vacation. Like Ocean Beach on a gray day. We're vacationing here in the fog.

You never completely figure Judy out. Lots of oppositions. I'm in love with her, I think; I think I love her and I wish she could love me. She's decided she's not going to love anyone for a while; she told me so. I keep hoping it might happen anyway.

Judy's in a bad mood today. I'm only catching parts of what she's saying because I'm thinking about a vacation she and Buster and I went on. Here's what I'm catching now: "...it's not a matter of figuring out what I want to do the most. I don't want to do anything. I've done enough things for a lifetime already. I'm sick of constructing a life just for something to do. Why not just forget it and skip the aggravation? It's all so annoying, all of it, every day, every decision, every breath—it's even an effort to breathe. They say that happens all by itself but it's a lie. Breathing's just another damn activity to fill up time and it's so fucked that we just can't turn it off when we don't feel like doing it. Being alive is like being a workhorse in a harness, plowing our way through the air until we die..."

This doesn't worry me. I'm used to Judy talking extremes to make a point. I wonder, though, if I missed the more casual part of this speech or if she just jumped right in at the life-is-fucked part.

Last spring the three of us decided to take a trip. I wanted to go someplace hot. Judy wanted to go somewhere clean and buildingless and relatively empty. Buster didn't much care. Actually, I just wanted to be with Judy somewhere different than here. We decided on White Sands, New Mexico, because Judy saw a picture and it looked like what she wanted. Clean and smooth. Only a little rise here, a cactus there. Mostly

The Wild Creatures

white sand. Symmetrical white emptiness. "Perfect," she said.

We took Judy's old station wagon. She seemed to relax as we drove along. Nothing to worry about. I drove most of the time and she'd put her feet up on the glove box, paint her toenails black, sing along with the radio and talk a lot to me or to Buster if she felt I wasn't paying attention. Buster always listens. I have a tendency to tune her voice out when she gets too cynical for too long. She doesn't really much care which one of us listens, she once told me, the talking's the important thing.

In the desert it got really hot and we'd ride along in just our underwear, or naked, sweating and drinking beer. It felt great. We didn't care if we ever got there because it was so fun riding naked and drinking beer all day. Buster was not as excited about the heat at first since he had nothing to take off, so I bought a block of ice for him and put it in the back of the station wagon. That way when he got hot he could go back and lie against it. Then when he felt cool he'd come back up to the front seat to his usual spot between Judy and me. He'd sit up and look out the front window, listen to Judy or the radio, and drool on the stick shift. Since he's shorter than us, from the back of the car we probably looked like a small family out on the road. That thought made me happy.

JUDY AT OCEAN BEACH: "We're slaves to life. That's all really. We eat, we shit, eat-and-shit and shit-and-eat like some disgusting mollusk, that's all. We're shithouses, storing it up until we overflow, until we explode with it. That's what happened to that guy this morning, he just exploded with it. I'm ashamed to be part of this mess but I don't have the guts to produce one more putrefying corpse out of myself to add to the heap. Besides I don't really see any difference between that and what all of us are now. Rotting matter either way. That's why we smell all the time, that's why everything that comes out of us smells, every labored breath smells. We're shit looking

71

Sam D'Allesandro

for a hole, that's all..."

White Sands was not quite as white or flat as Judy had hoped, not quite as smooth or devoid of human refuse; but she liked it well enough. It certainly was hot. Buster found a puddle around one of the camp faucets and stayed next to it all day so he could get in and cool off when he wanted to. Judy and I went for walks, sat in a spring drinking beer a lot, and got stoned to look at the stars. It can take a while to unwind. Toward the end, Judy was smiling and laughing more than I'd ever seen her. That's why I like to think about our vacation. Whenever Judy gets real depressed and starts talking too negative I think about our vacation at White Sands.

I wonder what might have set Judy's mood off today. Not that there has to be a reason. The guy across the street going crazy this morning could have done it. It seems like somebody goes crazy on our block about once a month now. I don't know what it is. This morning's broke out a couple of his apartment windows and then yelled and screamed for a couple of hours. About God, masturbation, his mother, his dead dog, things like that. When he got to the part about killing himself someone called the cops and they came over and put him in a paddy wagon. They put handcuffs on him. I could see Judy watching carefully from her window two floors above mine, watching to make sure the cops didn't hurt the guy or shove him or something when he was in the cuffs. Judy has a strong distrust of police. These were real gentle. They treated the guy like a baby, taking a long time to slowly walk him to the wagon, help him in, get him settled. As soon as they drove off Judy came down to see if I had caught all of this. We talked about it over coffee. I always think she looks beautiful in the morning, less tense. She showed me a letter to Ann Landers that began like this:

72

The Wild Creatures

Dear Ann Landers:

I am an eighteen-year-old single mother of twins. My parents threw me out of the house when I told them I was pregnant. Three months later after the twins were born I got herpes from a magazine salesman. The guy lied to me and said he had eczema. None of this has anything to do with my problem.

JUDY AT OCEAN BEACH: "...You know what I'd like? I'd like to find some place where everything we know about stops. I want to know what it's like to be able to stop everything without even the thought of starting it back up again. What it's like to stop and be stopped. Stillness without trying, without having to fight anything to make it happen. I want to know what it's like to be alone in an environment that doesn't include anyone else. Alone in the air. Just molecules. Just atoms. Just electricity. Just carbon. I want to unanimate myself for a while. To disassemble. I want to hear my brain stop communicating with itself..."

Just as the cops were leaving, Sammy, the fat guy who works at the corner store, came out and yelled hello to one of them. I guess he knew the cop from when he was the one that went crazy a couple of months back. He was February's crazy. The cop was laughing and yelled back, "I thought this call was probably to come and get you, Sammy." Sammy said no way. Then his mother came out to say hello to the cops too. She owns the store. Everyone calls her Mama. Mama was laughing and yelling back at the cops: "...not my Sammy this time, Sammy's a good boy now. Somebody else's kid this time. I call you next month to come and get Sammy again. Don't worry, I call if I need you." She was laughing and I could see her gold tooth from my window.

This all seemed pretty lighthearted compared to the middle of the night last February when it took four cops

73

to get Sammy into the car. Mama was screaming and wailing all night. Today when the cops drive off Mama just waves to Judy at her window and goes back in the store. Mama loves Judy. She calls her honey and she means it. Then everything was quiet. A little later, at Judy's, we can hear the building manager across the street sweeping up the glass from the broken window.

I'm thinking how quiet it was after the police left, after listening to the yelling and breaking glass all morning. No more yelling. No more glass. No more sirens. I wonder why people go crazy here. It's such a nice quiet block. It's by the park. When I have a day off and can stay home I find it very relaxing. If I was going to go crazy I'd be more apt to do it at work, or better yet in the subway, but here?—it's too calm. I wonder how anyone can get up such a head of steam in this neighborhood. I make a note to myself for later on to see what Mama thinks about this.

JUDY AT OCEAN BEACH: "...It's like this: my head is burning and I would like out. I don't want to die, I just want existing to be different. I want being alive to be different than it's seemed so far. What I'm looking for is something like what happens when, say, Maureen from The Velvet Underground hits that cymbal over and over just right. Or when PiL does 'Tie Me to the Length of That.' It's so perfect. Effortless. I want to be that effortless, perfect rhythm, that's all." (This is a good sign. When Judy starts getting poetic, it usually means she's winding down.) "Hey!—what in the hell's Buster got in his mouth...Buster, come here, come here, come show me that. God, Buster, that's disgusting."

She laughs. When Judy gets in these moods nothing I can say makes any difference. It used to make me feel inadequate. Then it dawned on me that she's actually talking more to herself than to me anyway. Like she said—the talking's the important part. Buster is the only one that can get her into a more playful world. I can wait

The Wild Creatures

while Judy goes through her rap a lot longer than Buster can. So I let him do the work. Then, slowly, she gets in a better mood and she's so beautiful to me, to me she's so beautiful I'm in love with her.

On the way home we walk past the cement wall that borders one side of the little baseball stadium. Letter by letter, we pass a long graffiti message written in one long line so that it takes about ten steps to reach each word. First message: T-H-E W-O-R-L-D I-S M-Y D-I-S-A-S-T-E-R. When we get to the last word Judy points to it and nods her head in agreement.

It's sunny now that we're away from the beach. We cast long funny shadows against the wall. We watch ourselves that way. A little further on another message begins: T-H-E W-O-R-L-D I-S M-Y C-O-M-P-R-O-M-I-S-E. I point the last word out to Judy. She rolls her eyes and smiles slightly.

Judy lets Buster run ahead of us. He hops along, flanked by a shadow much bigger than he is. The sun feels good radiating off the white wall and sidewalk. Everything slows down. It's a long block. Buster stops at a point in the distance. He's waiting patiently for us, sitting and facing the wall. I think he must be watching the little movements his ears make as he makes them go up and down in the shadow they cast against the wall. He seems to be concentrating, wrinkling and unwrinkling his forehead. If he were human his eyebrows would be moving up and down. When we catch up with him we see what he's looking at, a smaller graffiti message, written longhand in red letters: The World Is My Oyster. Buster cocks one spotted ear, angles his head in our direction, pauses for a moment, seems to wink, almost, then trots on, smiling the way dogs do.

Back from the beach, we buy burritos at a place near our building, smoke a joint, and sit up laughing. We're at Judy's place. We play "Tie Me to the Length of That" over and over on the stereo. Maybe twenty times. After about the tenth time it seems like maybe Judy's starting to get that rhythm she wanted. After about twenty times and another joint we're both in complete hysterics. Laughing hysterics, I mean. Buster eventually gets bored with this and curls up to sleep in front of one of the speakers. He doesn't seem to notice the noise coming out. Later I will go back down to my own apartment, I know, but not yet. It's another typical, wonderful day with my Judy, coming to an end. God, she's incredible.

Lenny

Lenny asked me to wait and I said, "I don't know." I really didn't, I was nervous, I'm not good at waiting, my confidence always sort of drifts off. I was holding his guitar. I watched him talking to somebody and a long line of sweat dripped down his leather pants, like a stripe, a black stripe, blacker than the leather, blacker than just black really because it was so shiny, blacker than anything, and then Lenny came back over. He was tired and smiling at me and he said, "Don't be so tough." I was scared.

I didn't know what he saw in me, I couldn't say anything, I was like a zombie, and he was hungry so we went to a drive-through. I spilled my milkshake on the floor of the car and then I had to go and bring up something about Patti calling me a faggot, that really pissed him off, he said not to worry about it—the milkshake on the rug that is. I wasn't really worrying about that.

Later, after, in bed, he said it was my eyes all along—my eyes all along, I couldn't believe he went after me just because he liked my eyes. Boy, he sure was skinny naked, but I liked it, he was so passionate and breathy and furry and when he took off his glasses he looked like a little mole or something—really vulnerable—squinting and all pale around the eyes, no, they were closed, actually they were closed the whole time, that's right, and he was just using his hands and those long fingers to see me with.

Giovanni's Apartment

He follows me all the way from the bus station to my neighborhood. It is late, almost no one out. When I turn around I can't see him but I know he's there. I can hear the click of his shoes against the sidewalk. I pass an old lady asleep in a doorway with a small gray cat. From the enormous pile of Macy's bags its green eyes blink up at me, offended and unfriendly, before returning to sleep. Cats used to come up to me. That seems to be happening less and less lately. All the dogs and cats I run into seem to be on a tighter schedule and have more of a destination mapped out than I do. I've been feeling more alone than when I first moved here and didn't know anybody. Now I know some people. That means I have less of an excuse to feel lonely but do anyway.

The feeling doesn't go away when, near the liquor store, a prostitute in spike heels and a big hairdo follows me for a block. Her smile turns venomous as we reach the intersection and I still haven't said yes. "Well, if you're not interested you could at least go to the liquor store and buy me a bottle of wine. Didn't your daddy ever teach you how to treat a lady, little boy?" She serves up that "little boy" with plenty of extra snide. I like her flair for the dramatic.

"Thunderbird 2000, that's all I want, baby." She's back to the sexy voice she used when she first approached me. As I get closer to the intersection it nose-dives into a grating, threatening whine: "Quit being such a pissant. You don't want to be a pissant all your life, do you?" I guess this barrage must have worked on someone for her to put so much effort into it, but I'm already blasé about anything anybody might say to me late at night around here.

In the middle of the next block I realize I can still feel

The Wild Creatures

him behind me, following in the distance. Even when I can't hear him I know he's there. I can feel him wanting me. As the gap between us gets smaller I start to feel what he wants to do to me. The whole hot scenario flashes through my mind, then starts to drop down through the rest of my body. A shivering wave of equal parts excitement and terror moves through my insides. I check to make sure the outside stays cool, stiffening all my muscles, especially my face. Guys like me mistakenly think that masks the vulnerability beginning to bubble up inside.

A block later he's ten steps behind me. "Are you gonna turn around and look at me?" The voice is low and quiet. It cements me to the square of sidewalk I'm standing on. I feel his eyes boring into the back of my head, making their way through a messy jumble of hair, skin, and tissue to an ugly unguarded place where thoughts are plainly visible. He stares at my fear and indecision like a grocery list. He's going shopping in there. I'm embarrassed to have him get behind my facade so easily, but there's nothing I can do about it. He's already inside where, at the moment, I'm nothing but a whirring mass of confusion and desire. He can see what's going to happen, what's possible with me. He can see which of the things he wants he can get.

Since I've been told to do so, in effect, I turn. I'm already giving him what he wants but that was going to happen anyway. I know that now, as my eyes check him out in nervous darts and jumps. You could make a picture out of the pattern my eyes follow as they scan his face, connecting from one point of interest to another, like a dot-to-dot drawn in by a hyperactive child. I mentally do so. The design hovers about an inch in front of his face for a moment.

That's the only way I can really get a good look at him, disconnecting the face and putting the image slightly outside so I can see it without getting caught. So

Sam D'Allesandro

I can look at it, recognize what it means to me, and then there's a feeling of giving into it as the picture hovers in front of him, slips away, and sinks back into the face it came from. He's solid again, 3-D and threatening. There's the hint of a smile on his lips.

I first saw that smile, that face, in a beautiful black-and-white film. When I mention it sometime later, he says he did it as a favor for a friend. He was never in another. The film lasts about forty minutes. In it he's almost a mannequin, his expression blank and unchanging as if it were painted on stone. He never speaks, although he's in almost every frame. The camera follows him as he walks all over a city. Which city isn't clear, as all the sites that could have distinguished it are left out. Dark and decaying urban neighborhoods, deserted blocks of apartment buildings, corner bars with tiny twenty-year-old neon signs, stores shut and barred. Everything looks fairly normal, fairly sinister.

He's wearing a gray suit, or one that looks gray in black-and-white. It's just rained and the pavement's slick and shiny. The only sound besides '50s jazz is the scrape and click of his shoes, snatches of disembodied voices drifting out from bars, a whoosh of tires against wet street in the distance. He moves through dark alleys, finally stopping at a door he seems to know. He knocks and, when a man comes to the door, he stabs him.

This is my first glimpse of Giovanni. It's the image I see in my head as we walk toward his apartment. I can't say whether I'm more attracted to the Giovanni walking beside me or the Giovanni/killer from the film. For me, so far, they're one and the same. I've actually spent more time observing the killer in the film than I have the flesh-and-blood person.

Over me washes a warm flush of fear and fascination with the possibility of my own violent demise. I think of

The Wild Creatures

the film, how easy it seemed to him. I imagine a few possibilities and prepare to die.

When he asks me my name, I stupidly shoot back, "Why do you want to know?" Instantly I wish I could grab the words back out of the air. Instead they hover there, naked and embarrassing, like a bad child I can't disassociate myself from. I watch him give an invisible mental snort, then drop the whole thing as if it hadn't happened. It's not really important to his plan, after all. So I give up and tell him.

We're still walking in my direction. I haven't had to make any turns yet that would show I'm leaving my route for his. From time to time a near-meaningless sentence falls out of my mouth.

"It's cold out tonight."

"Yeah, real cold."

He participates like a bad actor reading lines. We both know it's not necessary. Its main purpose—that of alleviating my nervousness—doesn't seem to be working. Besides, small talk sounds pretty silly when you put it alongside the thoughts running just beneath—both of us imagining a nakedness in the other we so far can't confirm. I know one thing he doesn't want—the me I appear to be to my friends. He wants a different me, naked and sweating and out of control, any iota of facade dissolved. And that's exactly what I needed. Even I know that now.

Inside my head I'm already beginning to imagine that I might be in love with him even as we're walking toward his apartment, toward his bed, his body. I'm already starting to see him as a warm, slightly frightening oasis against the backdrop of cold, dirty pavement, trash and leering car lights. Still walking, I watch the comparatively tiny practical portion of me tell the romantic side to shut up since it doesn't even know the guy.

Sam D'Allesandro

The pickup was that unremarkable. I was easy, but I had to be. I was a lonely, horny, walking bundle of need. I probably left a trail of the stuff on the sidewalk behind me like a snail slick. And everything about him worked: big enough, dark enough, demanding enough. There was no choice involved.

The bedroom had black walls. Red light coming from a lava lamp on the floor made it a warm and luscious hell. A fat mattress on a low platform was the only furniture I could see. I was alone: Giovanni had gone into the other room for something. As I lay down it was like sinking into a dream, deeper and deeper, until I disappeared into the bed. The red light turns to black. I sink in deeper still and my thoughts slow until almost motionless, until they begin to drown in heavy waves of barbiturate-like nothingness. Everything dissolves: me, the room, my mind. All my anxiety from meeting Giovanni slips away leaving me in sleepy comfort. I only want to stay there, deep in soothing folds of darkness and ready to sleep like a child in a warm bed on a winter night.

When I resurface he's standing over me, naked, watching. His skin is drenched in the red light, glowing with it. I reach my arms up toward his. We stay in this picture for some moments as he savors the exquisite little gulf between my gesture and his body. When he moves an inch closer, my hand runs slowly down his velvet belly, over the red-liquid skin, and I draw him to me. Then he kills me and revives me three times.

A month later he's everything. Everything about him is too good: the body, the apartment, the silence. The calm he puts inside of me like one long continuation of the feeling I had sinking into his mattress that first night—that was just a small taste of what Giovanni could be for me. Something important, primal, needed. He treated the animal side of me with the same care and nourishing a mother lavishes on a baby.

The Wild Creatures

Now I remember that actually I'd taken some codeine on my way home that night. I was looking for a little induced calm. Things hadn't been going so well and I needed to make my mind shut up for a while. But I forgot about that until sometime later, attributing all the dreaminess of the first night to Giovanni's efful- gence. By then he was installed inside me — the ultimate drug, effectively filling my bloodstream, warm and soothing, the thing that I wanted and knew I wanted. I loved knowing for a change.

I'm now thirty days old, all a continuation of that first night — hot bath, dream without end, big fat death of the outside world. He used sex as a means of commu- nicating. I need sex as a way to get into heaven. I didn't know exactly what I wanted, and what I needed I got.

He told me he had to be touching me in some way all night, or he couldn't sleep: an arm slung across my back, a leg twisted together with one of mine, a hand on my hip. Most of all he liked me curled into his furry gut, the smaller curve of my body swallowed by his larger one. Together we formed one large womb providing a safety neither of us possessed on our own. Not so completely, at least. I was shocked to think he needed me. I was willing to let him have whatever I had that he might want, but I wasn't sure what that might be. My attributes are invisible to me. The beauty he sees in me is different from that which I think of owning. He was falling in love with a person I didn't know and I was that person.

I stayed in the apartment for thirty-two days without leaving. I was swallowed. Day and night happened only indoors. The first day I almost made the conscious decision to take the day off, but it was more like I just didn't want to go to work; then I didn't go the next day, then never went again. It wasn't a good job anyway. The first morning, as he was leaving, he came back into the bedroom — dressed now in the gray '40s suit from the film, or one like it — leaned down, kissed me, and said,

Sam D'Allesandro

"Stay here, okay?" I remember lying in bed in the dark room and spotting the black telephone in the corner, with an answering machine attached. Its red-and-green blinking lights lit up a tiny portion of the darkness, maybe six inches square, reminding me of a miniature airport landing strip. I watched the little reds and greens for a long time, enjoying the warm dark, thinking about calling in, too lazy to get up, then too unconcerned. Then I never thought about the phone again for thirty-two days.

The living room was sunny and warm most of the day, sun streaming in through the windows. They looked out onto the interior of a block of houses and apartment buildings, the part where all the backyards meet inside the block. If I tired of sunbathing on the floor, I could go to the window and look out. Flowers, trees, dirt, garbage, a child's swing set but no child, two women having coffee at an iron table. I couldn't be bored. When even this simple panorama was too much for me to take in, I'd return to the bare symmetry of the sun-drenched floor. Even here the grain of the wood could fascinate or overwhelm me into shutting my eyes for a dreamless float. It's all I wanted. Something had happened to me, I knew, but I didn't know what and I didn't really care to know. It was something I'd needed for as long as I could remember, only I'd never known what or how to get it. Somehow Giovanni was making it happen, was giving me the life I'd never had.

  I lay on the floor as if it were a beach. The bedroom was always red and dark, each color dissolving into the other, always night — deep, black, and empty. That's the way I felt. It felt good. A lot fell away: my anxiety, my fear, my job, my apartment, my possessions, my need to create an existence. A new existence had already been created; all I had to do was slip into it. I started to feel alive again. My old life stripped away like dead skin. I

The Wild Creatures

abandoned everything that had happened before I met Giovanni. It disappeared. I was sick of carrying history around. If it had gotten me anywhere it was to Giovanni, and now that I was here I didn't need to know how it had happened. Sex was a way to forget. Each night, each time he killed me and revived me, a little more of my past slipped away, leaving me free to be happy for perhaps the first time ever. I loved the emptiness. I felt clean for the first time since I was born.

Giovanni let me do all this: stay in the apartment for thirty-two days; sunbathe on the living room floor all afternoon; drown in the red-black night of the bedroom; empty out, die, and revive three times each night. He let me do this because I wanted to. His only demand was for me to do as I wanted in the hope that it would always lead me back to him. I owned him now. I used sex to become exactly what he wanted. That was how I had captured him. I was his property now. He used sex to become exactly what I needed. We were deforming into Siamese twins.

As a child, I needed everything. I couldn't get anything from just being me. I couldn't masturbate. I couldn't sleep alone, I couldn't make decisions. I was a body looking for a schedule or set of instructions. I didn't know exactly what I should be wanting: I only knew how to be unsettled with what was happening around me but with no clue as to how to change that into something more satisfying.

I had one unbreakable routine. I sat around until no one was looking and then walked out the door. I kept walking until I somehow stopped: zombie-ing across intersections without looking, continuing over lawns, through vacant lots, housing-tract construction sites, shopping malls. If I hit a wall, I'd pivot like a robot and start in a new direction. I wasn't going anywhere in particular—I didn't care about destination. I wasn't thinking, I was just walking. I didn't know what else to

Sam D'Allesandro

do. At the time my actions seemed involuntary, now I'm not so sure. Of course I'd be tracked down eventually. It all depended on how much of a head start I had.

During the spanking with the spatula that always followed, I'm told that I stared blankly into space. And why not? After all, I hadn't been trying to be bad. It was out of my control. When the other kids on the block got bored, they found a new game or made a nuisance of themselves. I was different. I was ready to go out and find whatever seemed to be calling me out of the little house, away from my Tinkertoys and the two-toned TV set. It didn't matter if I found it. I was just a tourist at heart, a lost soul accidentally born on the wrong continent and trying to find my way back to Paris, a three-year-old sex slave looking for a master.

On the thirty-third day I went out—I was now thirty-three days old—the sidewalk felt like rubber, like a thin membrane floating on water. I wasn't sure I could move out of the way if someone came toward me. I wasn't sure I could speak. Staying in a quasi-controlled environment for thirty-two days has nothing to do with being outside. I was sure I couldn't have forgotten how to live outside the apartment but the sidewalk still felt like rubber.

I walked to the "dime store." Nothing there cost a dime. Even a #2 pencil was fifteen cents. I bought a package of small adhesive shapes that were made to glow in the dark after a light's been shone on them. The woman who sold them to me was a dwarf with blonde hair. She wore thick platform shoes to make her four inches taller. Even so, she still only came up to the level of my belly. As she rang up my purchase I suddenly had a paranoid vision of standing there blankly, unable to count out the money—like a three-year-old child. Indeed, as I lifted a handful of change toward her, most of it slid out of my hand and scattered onto the worn linoleum. She said, "Whoopsie daisy," the way my

The Wild Creatures

grandmother used to, the tone warm and meaningless, designed to make me feel more a victim of gravity than just plain clumsy. Her name was Mary. As she stooped to help me pick it up, I introduced myself and invited her to dinner the next night.

When she arrived the next night I was still on a high stool gluing the glowing shapes to the bedroom ceiling. I was making the Milky Way. Here I was God. I could recreate the star world any way I wanted.

Settling onto the bed below me, Mary kicked off her shoes, flipped her hair back out of her face, and told me she didn't usually accept dinner invitations from people she didn't know. "I have to be a little careful about people, being so small, but somehow I had a good feeling about you. I'm psychic, you know. I can usually trust my instincts about people. And you know what I thought about you? I thought, this guy doesn't need me for anything, he just wants company for dinner. A person who doesn't need you to be anything for them can be a good friend to have. So here I am. Actually I'm not as superstitious as this probably makes me sound. Besides, I never turn down a dinner invitation."

Far below me I could see her lying on the bed and talking. She looked even smaller than the day before. Without her shoes, her legs curled underneath her. For two hours she gave me suggestions about where to put the small glowing shapes, how a nebula should look, what parts of the Milky Way needed more filling in. From my perch I thought, *she certainly seems to know a lot about stars, she's a good person to have around at a time like this*. I could take her suggestions or not, she didn't seem to care. She kept on giving advice either way, another trait that reminded me of my grandmother.

"How about a supernova over there. No, more to the right. A little more...right there. Perfect."

I lay down on the bed with her and we turned out the lights. The blackness above became a sky, a black

87

Sam D'Allesandro

heaven with a thousand dots of green-white light, as if somehow I had covered the ceiling in a black sheet full of tiny pinholes and then shone a bright light above it. The room had changed, but then again it hadn't. It was still the black night it had always been, only more so. The feeling of sinking still soothed me. We lay on the bed for three hours. I told Mary about having not left the apartment for thirty-two days. She told me about her childhood.

Giovanni sat in the living room reading. Later the three of us ordered out for Chinese and watched David Letterman. Billy Idol was being interviewed, only he wouldn't answer any of the questions. He had his leather shirt open to the waist and kept sliding his hand inside to play with his nipples. Mary and Giovanni found this slightly shocking for TV. I didn't. Then Mary said goodnight and went home. Giovanni took me into the bedroom and killed and revived me three times under the stars. Afterward, he told me he loved me for making the bedroom into heaven. I loved him for making my body into heaven. It was now thirty-four days since Giovanni followed me. I was the same number of days old. Then I fell asleep and dreamed about Mary.

Here's part of what Mary told me that first night. Two days after her father tried to kill himself, her mother put her two children into the car and drove to the beach. Mary was five years old. The Santa Ana Freeway was bumper to bumper and it took hours to get there, hot and boring. The radio in the old Chevy was irritating with static but left on anyway, the same jingle repeating a hundred times: "One block Main Street, Santa Ana Freeway, Stanley's Chevrolet!" Other than that, no one said a word.

The Huntington Pier is long, old, and high above the water when you get out to the end. The three of them walk very slowly. The whole day seems as if it's happening in slow motion. Mary's mother wears a pink suit,

The Wild Creatures

something like the one Jackie Kennedy would make famous two years later in Dallas. In fact her mother looks something like Jackie Kennedy: dark shoulder-length hair, pink suit, medium high heels. Her face is beautiful and tense. They walk to the end of the pier and stand for a long time, not talking. Mary's mother holding each of their hands, one of them on either side. She's thinking. Anyone could tell. She's standing at the end of Huntington Pier where the water is very deep and the fishermen catch sand sharks and the barnacles on the pilings are said to be razor sharp.

Mary thinks about the one death she's already seen. She went fishing with her father and saw a girl jump off the pier here. The girl drowned. That day, her father stood, holding her hand, as they watched the Coast Guard cutter fish the body out of the water and bring it up to the aid station on the pier. Mary's thinking about that as she stands and watches the seagulls fight over little bits of bait and fish gut.

When she talks about that day now, her Jackie-on-the-pier story, she's got it down to one basic sentence: "There were gulls, fish smells, sun, a little breeze, and my mother in her pink suit holding her two children by the hands." One basic sentence for a scene that's flashed through her mind hundreds of thousands of times. "I understand what happened. I just don't know what it means.

"When my father came out of the hospital a year later, he rented a hotel room and stayed there for six days. He killed himself with a mixture of valium, Gordon's gin, and hypothermia. He passed out in a tub of cold water and his body temperature dropped until he died. When I was older, and my mother told me how he'd done it, I imagined him frozen from the inside out. She said his heart just stopped beating."

This is the story Mary told me the first night she came over, one day after I met her and thirty-four days after I met Giovanni.

The only people I know now are Giovanni—the man who followed me—and Mary. I never told anyone where I'd moved. I never went back to my old place; I didn't want anything there. Everything I needed was here. About the third day, Giovanni asked me if I needed anything from my old place. We were sitting at the little dinette table in the tiny room full of windows between the kitchen and the living room. I was wearing his plaid shirt. "No, nothing," I said. "I mean, you don't have a cat or anything?" *No*, I thought back, remembering, *I don't*. Dino was dead. I shook my head. "Good." That was the end of it.

I was still wearing Giovanni's clothes, only now it didn't seem like I was wearing someone else's clothes. Now they were just our clothes. That sounds silly, but the fact is we were both wearing them, every day. I never returned any of the phone calls to those friends that found out where I'd moved to. I let the machine talk instead. They were not my friends anymore. They were friends of someone they remembered me to be that I wasn't anymore, or maybe never had been. I'd never had that many friends anyway. Now as I moved about the apartment every other day or so the phone rang three times, then the message went off, then a maybe distantly familiar voice might say my name, leave a number, and hang up. As time went on this happened less and less.

On Sundays the three of us took Mary's one-eyed, no-tail dog, Barney, for walks in the park, or sometimes a picnic. Tuesday nights we'd go to Charlie's to watch Giovanni shoot pool. I loved holding the shiny glass balls in my hands. Sometimes I'd slip one in Mary's purse when no one was looking and take it home. Mary would roll her eyes at the theft in a slight bit of disapproval, then say nothing and walk out. In a way she was as attracted to the pool balls as I was, delighting

The Wild Creatures

in the growing collection. Mary attracted things anyway, all sorts of things, accumulating and stacked into her upstairs apartment over the dime store. Giovanni and I had almost nothing. Gio liked it spare, minimal, clean. A big pile of colored pool balls sat in one corner of the living room.

Coming into the kitchenette area one day, Mary spotted her mother languishing with coffee at the metal dinette table. Occasionally she brushed the hair out of her eyes with her hand. She was reading a stack of colorful magazines and smoking a cigarette. The effect was stunning, the style and positioning of the elements in the pose an almost unbelievably glamorous combination, so self-absorbed, so eloquently casual. A perfect laziness. "Maybe she's eating a little square pan of fudge with a spoon," Mary told me. "I can't recall." For a long time after this we steal cigarettes from the neighbors' house and lay them out with a magazine on the dinette, hoping to entice Mary's mother to repeat her impressive carelessness.

Sitting at the kitchen table, smoking a cigarette, with the latest issue of *Vanity Fair*, I try to imitate the way Mary remembered her mother looking that day. I drink more coffee. I try slumping more. I take another drag on my Salem, but her study in coolness escapes me. I'm a million miles from the image, from the experience I'm after. Maybe the magazine isn't trashy enough to make me not care about anything, to induce the total laziness. I wonder if possibly a hangover Mary never knew about is supposed to be part of the scene. Maybe it's the missing pan of fudge that's keeping the whole attitude from solidly setting in.

At some point, Giovanni decided the apartment had become too cluttered and he systematically began removing things, maybe one every other day. At first I hardly noticed. I didn't really know where these things went until one day Barney and I stumbled over our portable TV outside. I guess Giovanni had been putting the stuff out on the sidewalk free for anyone who wanted it. *That's Gio*, I thought to myself. I picked up the little TV and took it to Mary's. I had the key.

After a while there was nothing left in the apartment except the mattress in the bedroom, the lava lamp on the floor next to it, the dinette in the kitchen, and the Saturn chair in the living room. I didn't mind so long as he didn't throw out anything Mary had brought over. Next, the few things left started moving from room to room. One day the mattress was in what used to be the bedroom, then in the living room, maybe in the dining room a week later. As the mattress moved, the dinette and Saturn chair usually moved too. The rooms didn't really have names any more, except the bathroom. They were all just empty spaces. Boxes. I had to look each day to see where things were, but that wasn't too hard since there weren't many things and I wasn't doing anything but reading the paper and walking Barney anyway. I never asked him why he was doing it. He wanted to.

Then one day I realized that the phone no longer worked. It had been so long since it rang that I'd stopped thinking about it. I'd always let the machine answer anyway since the only one I wanted to talk to besides Giovanni was Mary, and she never called, she just came over. Or left a note. "Come by the store." I don't know when it stopped working.

Slowly I began to realize that Giovanni no longer had any friends besides Mary and me. At least not any that would come over. He always had before. I guess he spent so much time with us now they had just fallen away.

At first this bothered me a little. I didn't really know what was going on but I didn't want to ask. I wanted to just let him go through whatever it was he was doing. After all, he'd let me do whatever I wanted without

The Wild Creatures

question, as long as I was still there for him. I stopped thinking about it and listened to the radio more. At first I was bored. Then I stopped wanting to do anything else. Then it became satisfying. Listening to the radio seemed to be what I was supposed to do, so I was doing it.

I went out less and less, not wanting to move away from the radio on the living room floor. Giovanni took over some of Barney's walks. The rest of the time Barney would sunbathe with me on the living-room floor. He was old. Mostly he just slept or else listened to the radio too. I could tell he liked certain songs more than others. Chaka Khan was his favorite.

By this time Gio and I thought I must be going a little crazy again. Except for occasional short walks with Barney, I was going into another thirty-two-day hibernation. I was the one going crazy since the only thing I wanted to do was listen to the radio. Giovanni wasn't crazy for taking all the furniture out of the apartment and never speaking. I was crazy for living in an apartment that had no furniture with someone who never spoke.

We still made love every night. Amazing, terrific killings and resurrections, night after night. Those were the only sounds we made with each other. It was the only exercise I got. I could feel my legs and back and arms stretching, feel air coming into my comatose lungs. For the first time all day we'd be really looking at each other, our lips brushing, not able to get enough of each other, petting hair and arms and stomachs as if each of us were a little baby with the mother he totally loves and who totally loves him more than anyone else in the world. We were using sex to be together. Once in a while, at these times, I would whisper his name, just to make sure I still had it.

I lived on coffee and cereal. That's all I would eat. Plus a big bowl of vitamins left by the bed for me each morning with a note that said, "Eat these." Giovanni

Sam D'Allesandro

must be the one leaving them, but I was asleep so I don't know for sure. This went on for I don't know how long. Maybe if I'd felt I was in jail I'd have made marks on the wall to count off the days but I didn't so I didn't. Giovanni now took Barney for all of his walks. The front door was unlocked but I wasn't sure if there was a world beyond it anymore or, if so, what kind of world it was. I knew there must be a world that Giovanni went out into every day, but I wasn't sure that I could do the same. I pictured it as a membrane that you had to try and walk through. If it accepted you, you reached another place outside the apartment. If not, it bounced you back hard onto the floor, leaving you dazed and feeling something was wrong. Inside the apartment nothing was wrong. It was my world, the warm living-room floor and the soft radio. Perfect. Everything just as it should be. I ate my vitamins, had coffee and cereal, petted Barney, followed the sunny spots on the floor around the living room, listened to the radio, and made love at night.

One night Barney woke me up to show me a mouse in his water dish. Apparently it had tried to get a drink, fell in, and drowned. Barney and I lay down on the cool linoleum and looked at the little mouse body for a long time. Then Barney fell asleep.

From where I lay I could see the dinette table where Mary and I had worked so hard at recreating the smoking-Jackie image her mother had once evoked: silver legs, mosaic surface of grays and dirty rose, metallic chairs covered in metal-deck vinyl. I think those chairs were the only furniture Giovanni ever spent money on. A big sculpture of Barney made out of insulating wire hung above the table. I made that, a long time ago it now seems. If you follow the wire Barney to the ceiling, and let your eye travel down and around the bend of the doorframe into the kitchen, you come to a yellowed and grease-spattered de Kooning print, the shiny paper now dull and thick. It's an ad for his Grand

94

The Wild Creatures

Palais show in Paris, 1979: a woman with blonde hair and two big eyes, one bigger than the other, one set higher than the other. She could be Mary. In the painting you can't tell how tall she is. A series of slashing lines and scribbles takes your eyes down to enormous breasts, barely covered by what looks like a pink cocktail dress, down past the triangular crotch with the extra line accents, past the type that actually advertises the show, to the white slick of the refrigerator.

My eyes stop when they get to the messy patchwork of newspaper clippings that Mary and I put up with the little black magnets she stole from the dime store. Off to one side is a lime green religious tract that an old lady once handed me on the street. I lie on the cold linoleum listening to the refrigerator hum and Barney sleeping and go over and over the words:

> *You probably had a normal childhood. No major worries; no struggle for existence. And there were some high points: the first job; courtship and marriage; a new home; the first child.*
>
> *But now days pass by in monotony. So you shop aimlessly or watch TV or find hobbies. Some try divorce or alcohol. But nothing is solved.*
>
> *You see the neighbors in the same rut. There's no future except routine, then old age. Then death. And that's scary!*

I was still lying there with Barney when Mary came in. It was just starting to get light. She'd used her key, not wanting to wake us. She'd just got back and couldn't wait to see Barney. Mary didn't say a word about finding me naked on the kitchen floor, she just leaned down (which wasn't very far for her) and kissed me on the cheek. Sleepy Barney suddenly jumped up and started dancing around her, his toenails making a racket of little clicking sounds on the linoleum, snuffling and snorting and making whining noises as Mary petted him.

"Go get your clothes, and we'll take Barney for a walk. How's Gio?"

"He's okay."

"What happened to all the furniture? Never mind. Your TV's sitting on my coffee table. At least you still have the Saturn chair and the dinette. My God, I've got to be able to sit down somewhere when I come visit."

"Mary..."

"You know what I wanted to do? I wanted to come in this morning, see Barney, and then crawl into bed with you and Gio. I missed you guys so much. You'd have been so surprised. I don't know, though, I might not have had the guts. I've never even seen Gio naked. Wait a minute, yes I have, that night I brought over the martinis and he was in the tub so we went in and sat around drinking martinis. That was so fun. How could I forget it. I even told my mother about that. I told her all about you two."

Barney trotted along in front of us sniffing invisible things of apparent importance. He hardly ever looked up; his eyes were always glued to the two inches of ground in front of his nose. It was cold out, leaves on the path. I hadn't realized that in the last forty-nine days the seasons had begun to change. It seemed like summer the last time I was out. Perhaps knowing I hadn't spoken in a while, Mary did all the talking, rattling on, jumping from one subject to another, then back to a previous one. When she really got going, you had to know Mary pretty well to follow. When Giovanni first met her, he'd ask me later what she was talking about. I'd tell him how she got to topic K from topic Z, and what K had to do with H, and how she got to H from A. Once you got to know Mary's mind, how quickly it moved, you learned to follow. You had to adopt her logic. If I'm around Mary all day I sometimes notice that I'm starting to think and sound like her. That means no one else will be able to

The Wild Creatures

follow me except Mary and Giovanni. Maybe Barney—I'm not so sure about him. But they're the only ones I talk to anyway.

I'm thinking about this as we walk and Mary continues to rattle. She hardly stops for a breath, occasionally reaching—she doesn't need to stoop—to give Barney a pat. After forty-eight days in the apartment, the streets are almost unbearably beautiful. I finally manage to speak, wedging in when Mary takes a breath. I tell her about Barney waking me up to show me the mouse in his water dish.

"He'll never drink out of that dish again. He's like that. Once he found a cricket swimming in his old dish and that was it. He never went near it again. Too bad, that Yogi Bear dish was pretty cute too."

Then I tell her about Giovanni throwing out all the furniture except the Saturn chair. Mary laughs and when I say "No, I'm really kind of concerned," she stops walking and takes both my hands.

"Listen, that's just Gio. He needs a change once in a while. He goes to work five days a week. He likes his work but gets a little freaked playing Mr. 9-to-5 sometimes, that's all. Didn't you ever think he maybe needed to do something to compete with your spells? He loves you. If you go crazy he'll take care of you for the rest of your life. And it's not just a physical thing—all that killing and reviving you talk about—it's deeper. He's not a talker. He just wants to feel it and do it. He doesn't say it, he shows it. And that's pretty great. So don't worry. The apartment's beautiful empty, you have to admit—good floors, good light. It'll fill up again. I'll fill it, slowly so as not to cause a stir, one thing at a time. My place is so crammed I've got to farm the stuff out somewhere. Besides, I'm giving up my storage bin at U-Haul. I'm sick of paying the damn rent on it."

I didn't even know Mary had a storage bin. Then she lowers the boom. She thinks it's time for me to get a job.

Sam D'Allesandro

Her words send a stinging sensation of violent fear up my spine to my head. A shiver runs through my brain, vibrates off the top of my head, and is gone.

"Just something part-time, no big deal. I'll help you find something in the neighborhood to start with." The fact is Mary already knows of a job opening at the place where we buy our coffee. This seems perfect to her because the hours wouldn't conflict with our morning visits. And we'd also be able to get free coffee. Mary, in her own way, always thinks things out logically.

"But what about *The Flintstones* in the afternoon?"

"Come on, I think we've seen enough of those to last a lifetime. Really, don't you think you're ready for this? I do. You can't do thirty-two days in this apartment again." (I didn't tell her it had actually been forty-eight by this time, more or less.) "You needed to do that, that's okay, but now you're through it. Let's face it, it's time, sweetie."

Unbelievably I somehow found all this making some kind of vague sense. I quietly began mulling over the image in my mind, picturing myself behind the coffee-store counter, wearing one of their dark green aprons, measuring out fresh beans into the grinder. In my mind, the other people who worked there seem pretty hip. And the place always smells good. Mary took my silence as a good sign and shut up for a while.

By the time we get back to the apartment, Giovanni's gone and I've pretty much snapped out of my forty-eight-day torpor. It happened that fast. I show Mary the tract on the fridge that possessed me the night before.

"Hmm, maybe we should drop that from the collection. It gives me the creeps."

The espresso pot's already rumbling on the stove. This causes Barney to retreat into the other room as usual. Once we're settled in at the dinette with our coffee, Mary begins again:

"You know she's not coming out this time, my

The Wild Creatures

mother. Our Jackie doesn't look too good. By the time I got there she'd already gone back into the hospital. I went in and—you know, she's not really our Jackie anymore at all. She's lost a lot of weight. She's got about four inches of gray roots showing. Almost white. In the last six months she's aged about ten years. Somehow she got old. Somehow I didn't think that would ever happen.

"She was asleep. I sat with her a long time. Then she woke up and we talked for a while. She's pretty weak but she was really happy to see me. She asked about you and Barney and Gio. When it was time to go I told her not to worry, she'd be out in a couple of days. She said, 'No, honey, not this time. I'm going to die soon, Mary. If I get out I won't get out for long.'

"I'm going back down in two weeks, after I get things squared away here. Will you come down with me, at least for a while? She wants to meet you. I told her about us reenacting the Jackie-at-the-dinette scene and she thought that was hysterical. I've got to go. She doesn't need me, it's not that, she's still the totally self-contained phenomenon she always was. It's just—I don't know, she's the one I always wanted to be. I want to see her a little more before she's finished being perfect."

Giovanni comes too, and Barney. For the weekend. Then I have to get back to start my new job. It's only part-time. Giovanni looks on it as an amusing experiment. He really doesn't care if I do it, he just wants me to do what I want to do. But I'm ready, and Mary wants me to do it. She made me promise to at least give it a try. I also have the job of painting her apartment while she's gone. I suspect it's just a ploy to keep me busy. She's going to give me $200 and I'll buy Giovanni a VCR for Christmas. Then we can all watch *The Flintstones* and *Our Miss Brooks* reruns at night. Except Tuesdays, cheap beer night, Gio's pool night.

1960

When I was four my family moved out of a wonderful house. It was in a row of adobe houses a block from the beach, all painted blazing white in the Los Angeles sun. They looked like a Greek island village or someplace in Sicily. The houses were very old. Every once in a while, one of them would cave in and so they became condemned. We had to leave our simple life in the beach ghetto.

But we were lucky. We were able to grab a piece of America by the tail, a piece of the pie, some of that American-dream action we all knew we'd get if we worked hard—and we had—so God rewarded us. We moved into a tract house. It had the greenest snow-pea green stucco all over it that would alternately crumble off in our hands or rip our fingers to shreds if we fell against it while playing. Another amazing thing—the tract house had gravel instead of a lawn. I used to love looking for rare rocks in the gravel and I made a collection of them in a cigar box my father gave me.

So here we were in this incredibly compartmentally ugly L.A. suburb living the good life. I remember several things about life there. I remember my cat, Daniel Boone, got hit by a car and broke his leg. I found him in the garage with blood on his mouth, but he didn't die. He got a cast instead, a cat cast. He would always get stuck in what neighborhood trees there were since he could climb up with the cast but not down. I remember my mother appearing one day with a new baby she said was my brother. I don't remember her being pregnant; she just showed up with this baby. I also remember my mother making my sister and me walk from house to house when we first moved in asking if they had any kids our age to play with. We were more than embar-

The Wild Creatures

rassed. We didn't want to play with any kids who would respond to such a tactic anyway.

I remember the neighbor across the street had a wooden leg. One day he took it off and showed it to me. And I remember the neighbors next door had a luau. Those were "in" that year. All the women wore muumuus. I remember our tract went heavily against Kennedy for Nixon. It was 1960 and none of us knew anything of what we would learn in the next ten years.

I liked Wagon Wheels. Wagon Wheels was a snack, really just raw macaroni in a nice box, but I liked it and always tried to get my mother to buy me some. She wouldn't. I would whine about those Wagon Wheels until my mother would spank me with a pancake turner, the favorite weapon of the neighborhood mothers.

One night my sister and I were sitting at the serving bar that separated the pastel kitchen from the gaudy living room when my sister absently knocked the newspaper onto the electric range below. I watched it catch fire. I watched it start to flame. I was enthralled as it was the first range-fire I had ever witnessed. My mother and sister were both standing right there but didn't seem to notice the flames now leaping from the range. I guess they were thinking about something else.

Finally my surprise at their lack of interest got the best of me so I pointed the paper out to them. Now my mother did seem interested after all. She yelled for my father and my father came running in naked and all wet, from the bathtub and, for a moment, my first experience of true pandemonium occurred. It was fairly short-lived. Soon my father had smothered the fire with his bath towel. As a reward for spotting the fire, my mother bought me a box of Wagon Wheels. I remember a happy afternoon spent sitting on the front step eating my Wagon Wheels and watching the traffic. This was one of my first encounters with life's system of rewarding the obvious rather than the extraordinary.

Sam D'Allesandro

One day my sister went to a Barbie Beauty Contest at Brownies. The most beautiful Barbie doll would be crowned queen of all the other Barbies. My sister came home crying with her Barbie in its little Barbie wedding dress jammed into a sack. My mother tried to calm her down and find out what was the matter. What was the matter was that all the other girls had told my sister that her Barbie was the ugliest of all. How she cried. Later she would become a beautiful woman—picture a powerful, successful executive who makes lots of money—but that hadn't happened yet. For now she just cried and cried.

We moved not too long after that. I never lived in a housing tract again, but I never forgot the lessons I learned there. A plague of confusion has followed me ever since.

Walking to the Ocean This Morning

The truth of the matter is I like to be beaten and then fucked like a dog. I don't just mean on my hands and knees, I mean hard and carelessly. I want someone relentless. When I was with Tom, before, saying no in the morning could easily be followed with a slap in the face and a spanking so hard it would send me crawling from room to room looking for escape in fear of even being touched on my now-burning ass, until he would decide to catch me and fuck me roughly on the floor. I'd start out whimpering and end up moaning within minutes. Once he had me in that place, he liked to threaten to stop just to hear me beg him not to. Tom loved to create situations that would totally turn what I thought I wanted at that moment to the opposite, from saying I didn't want to have sex that morning to begging him not to stop fucking my spanked ass. He didn't force me to do anything, he just created situations in which I wanted what he was going to give me anyway. Sometimes he'd fuck me real hard and then pull out, holding my legs straight up in the air in a flying V, looking at my enlarged asshole sucking air to fill the vacancy, begging for his cock to return. I loved being so vulnerable. I loved it when my tits or my cock or my asshole would destroy my own ego with their needs. If your body wants something bad enough, you can't say no no matter how humiliating. He could say anything, call me anything, make me do anything, after which I would immediately start begging for his cock. At those moments I didn't matter, only my ass did.

The Zombie Pit

Last night at a local bar, crowded and loud, Sid and I were the most entertaining of all those vying for public attention. I can't remember all the details but later we debated a dim memory of my cock becoming exposed and whether I or someone else was responsible. My jeans have a seven-inch slice in the left rear-thigh zone and someone kept reaching inside, the hand unknowingly edging up toward the diagonal scar that cuts through my left cheek. A finger traced the ruby-ridged edge, curious and finding out. I liked that.

On the way out, I ran my hand around the narrow waist and over the gentle belly of the boy who'd been flirting from across the bar. I had danced with him a year earlier at a big party because the glint of gold through such a young nipple stopped me in my tracks. But he wouldn't kiss me. This time I tell him, "I would have been your slave." I don't know why I say it since I don't really mean it. I just want him to think about the possibility. I don't wait for his reaction. I'm counting on not running into him for another year, that's how long it took last time. I think he's trouble, but he reminds me of someone in New Orleans, the one with the scars. And then I go all sloppy inside.

I'm naked right now. I'm dripping wet, just out of the shower. I've got a cup of Ethiopian Mocha Harrar espresso and I'll kill anyone that tries to take it away from me. Sid left my bed exactly ninety minutes ago. In that time it takes to watch most American movies, I slept some more, made coffee, opened the blackout curtains, took a shower, and borrowed a porno magazine from my roommate's bedroom. And I actually did it right over the magazine; I found the picture I wanted and I couldn't stop staring at it—everything just right and all—until I'd made a ruin of it. Later that will smear and either stick the pages together or else take the ink right off the sheet. Either way, what was perfect for me this morning will be gone.

Last night when the bartender asked Sid and me what we wanted ("Anything," we said) we thought it was free. That was wrong, but I guess it figures that reading a hulking guy named "Gidget" might be confusing. I still think we were being pretty entertaining. I remember being on the floor at some point but not how I got there. Also biting someone hard in the urinal, the trough that is. Maybe that was Sid. Or maybe it was the one flirting from across the bar, the one with the gold ring in his nipple. The one that looks like but isn't the one with the scars. Farrell.

I'm telling you about Farrell because he's the opposite of Sid. He's so physically and sexually perfect for me that his failure in other areas is irrelevant. I can imagine living on welfare in an East L.A. barrio for him, just so I can be near him as he sleeps at night. I'm four years younger. It's hot. A slight, barely cool breeze occasionally stirs the curtains around the open window. Outside a tiny backyard connects to an alley connected to the rest of Los Angeles. He's naked, a wadded sheet entwining one leg and swathing the tan skin of his lower belly in white. The legs are long and akimbo. Arms reach up to clasp hands under his head, the dark hair in the armpits thick and curling with sweat. Tiny beads cross his smooth forehead.

I want to lick him all over. I pet the dark hair that covers his legs and fills the groove running down the center of his chest. I move on top of him, pressing my body so close that it melds to his. A rupture opens in the long torso. I pour into it. I'm taken, somehow, inside of him—sinking in until I disappear. My fears, insecurities, dissatisfactions all melt, until he's left sultry and alluringly alone on the bed. Simple and solitary.

Sam D'Allesandro

None of this happens since I'm afraid to chance waking him. I'm sitting against the wall in the room's gray light, staring first at him, then out the open window into the L.A. night, then back at him.

Now I've let you in on one of my secret parts.

A different image appears. One that only Farrell and I can see exactly. A scene played over another cup of coffee laid out on a slightly grimy Formica table in West Hollywood. It starts like this: "Listen, not everything I say to you relates only to the fact that it's being said to you. Some of it relates to me!"

He continues to stare out the window, stirring his coffee like a beautiful mechanized art piece animated for table amusement. A perfectly emotionless robotron. Annoyed with the vision and how much I want him anyway, I continue, even though I know we'd probably both be a lot better off if I'd just shut up now. I watch helpless as my mouth opens and develops my simple pronouncement into an ugly tirade. "Let's face it. The self-indulgence I like best is my own. I'm the most important person in my head—I have to be. That's not self-indulgence anyway, that's survival, believe me, no one else, no one, cares that much whether I manage to stay intact or not. Least of all you."

Two weeks later you would have thought I was responding to a totally different person. Actually it was just his other side coming out, like *The Three Faces of Eve*. (Strange that Sid would later refer to me as the One Hundred Faces of Eve.) This time it's his busy-betty tyrannical half rather than the who-cares autonomy of two weeks earlier. In the Three Faces of Farrell, I suppose the third face would have to be his face itself. Farrell as angel. Farrell as a perfection I could never leave. Only, I did.

Before I left I finally had to say this: "I love whatever it is you are to me, but one thing that it's not is my mother. There won't be another mother in my life, ever.

106

The Wild Creatures

I am she, my own best superego in a constant and spectacular smashup with an impulsively conniving id. Just pieces of things, really, in pretty active disagreement. That's who you've been dealing with. That's what you've been up against."

That left him speechless. I didn't expect a big response; after all, I was the wordy one, while he was the one with the sultry, accusing looks. Still, he knew I only meant about half the intensity my tone implied. It was basically nothing more than a thin attempt at defense since if he had asked me to stay I would have.

Four years after leaving Farrell in L.A., what I want to know about Sid is whether he hates me or just wants to fuck me. There was a time when I believed everyone divided into those two categories. Poor Sid doesn't deserve that, but the fact is it's still there. One way or another he'll have to deal with it.

Over coffee at Corbas I tried to explain to my friend Ed.

ME: Yesterday my glasses broke and then two people started crying for different reasons. One because his best friend is dying. The other because I don't love him anymore. Actually I do love him, just not in the way he wants. I love somebody else that way, the one whose best friend is dying. Sid.

(In spite of the shower, coffee, masturbation, and day off, so far I'm irritable. I know if I can find someone to take it out on I will. Until I find that someone Ed is getting to be therapist instead. Outside the café there's a horrible woman walking down the street with a birdcage in her hand. Suddenly everything's overcast. The sun's gone and I blame her.)

ME: Later I have to go out and buy a birthday present—an expensive one is expected, I know. I also have to buy a can of paint, a piece of plywood, and groceries. That's the kind of life I lead these days. Task-

107

Sam D'Allesandro

level, that's me.

Lately I keep telling everyone, it's me you have to like, me, not some image that I can project or that can be projected on me. Eventually those all fall apart, under duress. Know what I mean? Like on *20/20* last week. Look at the difference between Elvis in that all-black skintight leather suit on his 1966 TV special, and those sickeningly bloated, barely predeath pictures they kept showing of him when Barbara Walters was interviewing Priscilla Presley, who actually looked like a Filipino drag queen in the old pictures herself. See what I mean? It's the same Priscilla Presley whether looking like a 1966 drag queen or a beautiful forty-year-old passing for thirty on *Dallas* twenty years later. The same Elvis thin in sleek black leather as the post-Liberace nightmare we saw ten years down the road. It's the same me, no matter what image I try to take on or what anyone else wants me to be. [*Pause.*] Actually I haven't been saying that to everyone, only to one. Sid.

Right now I feel swollen, like I'm a depressed fifteen-year-old again, only I'm not depressed, just emotionally exhausted. Tired of thinking. Tired of talking just to talk. And of course that makes Sid think that I'm either depressed or that I no longer like him.

I keep wondering if I stop talking and being active and laughing if he'll go away. Sid, I mean, the one whose friend is dying. It's not that I want him to. It's just that unless he'll stay with me no matter what I figure he won't stay. Someday he'll go.

ED: If you stopped being active and talking and laughing I guess it would be the same as you going away for Sid. Emotionally at least.

ME: I never think of me leaving. I only think of Sid leaving me.

ED: He's probably the same way. Why don't you stop thinking about this relationship so much and just sit back and enjoy it a little? He seems to be the one you want.

The Wild Creatures

ME: If you really want to know, he's all wrong. He's too happy. He's always smiling and friendly to everyone. Everyone. You can't trust what's really going on beneath that. Besides, it makes me feel socially inadequate. I like brooders.

ED: You mean the ones you see leaning against a wall looking overly serious?

ME: Right.

ED: Actually, except for you, the person I know that sounds the most like is Sid.

Sid. He has a fear of fading into the background. He's either handsome in a quirky kind of way or he's not handsome, I can't tell anymore. He dresses strangely — he doesn't think carefully about what he's doing, yet he always stands out. People stare at him in elevators and on the subway without quite knowing why. He doesn't look that odd. He's often slightly overformal in casual situations, but in a messy sort of way: the black shoes scuffed, the shirt unironed, the tie not quite knotted right.

When I met him, the things that stuck out in my mind were that 1) he made me laugh on a very bad day without pulling me out of the mood I needed to be in, and 2) he had the absolute messiest apartment I had ever seen. In the beginning I wanted not to care too much and just allow Sid to entertain me. That was only fair since he seemed to be entertained by me. Now I care a lot. A month after I met him he bought me a lava lamp named Sperm. Red lava bubbling in amber liquid. It lives in my room on the night table.

At different times Sid relaxes, excites, agitates. He splurges on Sushi Gen when all I really wanted was a hamburger, likes to see me cry but doesn't like to make me cry, gives me a hundred kisses when I'm sad. He works in a coffee store and gives me half pounds of Kona and Ethiopian Mocha Harrar, the most expensive beans sold, for free.

ED: Which do you like the best, the coffee or the man who sells it?

ME: I like the man who sells it best, but best of all I like the one who sells it bringing me a cup afterward.

The first time I saw Sid was at the Pyramid Club in New York two years ago: he's dancing with a girl in an aqua minidress and short black hair. She's smiling at him. She grabs his hands for a moment and then releases them with a little whirling circle around her spot on the fluorescent-paint-spattered floor. She does that over and over. Grabbing, releasing, grabbing, releasing. At one point there's even a quick little red-lipsticked kiss that leaves Sid looking either funny and devil-may-care or stupid and silly.

Then she crumples to the floor, eyes closed, head thudding audibly over the blare of the speakers, legs bent and curled to one side. Her arms splay awkwardly in the opposite direction. She's so tiny that kneeling over her Sid looks like Godzilla. When her foggy eyes begin to clear, she reaches up and slaps him hard. The second swing comes even harder as her efforts regain focus: eyes flashing, mouth spitting and screaming, nails out and digging into the skin of his cheek. A layer of fleshy meat peels away, leaving a long, irregular red stripe. By the time the bouncer arrives, another woman has dragged her panting and crying to the aluminum-foil-covered bathroom. The bouncer asks no questions, pushing Sid out to the street with a threat and a kick.

It took another year after that for Sid and me to both wind up in the same city and bother to get to know each other. Now it's like this, like the way I've been describing. Indefinable, already important, vaguely trap-like.

Before I met Sid, I used to walk around talking to Farrell all the time, as if he were right there beside me rather than vanished from the face of the earth. I said lots of things I hadn't been able to say when we were together. It was like a trance: I didn't hear other people, didn't see other people. Everything outside of my head had stopped, for about a year, year and a half.

I rode the subway a lot. If you stand at the front of the front car you can stare out the front window as it speeds along through the tunnel. It's just blackness. Occasionally there's a few little green or red lights, just specks, like fireflies, and some dimly lit gray spaces that could actually be a horrible little world where someone might be living. But I liked that blackness, that was the part that soothed me.

My money ran out and I had to get a job in a diner for a while. Bee's Coffee Cup. The first real voices I'd heard in a long time were saying things like "Can I have some more coffee?" Just these customer voices. Just little sentences that didn't mean anything except exactly what they said. "More coffee?" — more coffee.

"Can I have some more coffee?"

Looking up, the first thing I noticed was that his hair matched the little buttons on my black coat. Black-black, not just dark brunette. Then the scene from the Pyramid Club popped into my head. For the moment, I kept that knowledge to myself. I wasn't used to talking much anyway. By the end of a short, mostly one-sided conversation, Sid was an address on a torn piece of paper I'd probably lose by the time I got home. Somehow he managed to escalate it from there.

Early Sid and me:

"I need something primitive. Like my friends, Dick and Sally. When they're angry they scream at each other. If she's mad at him she withholds sex and if she's happy with him she cooks bigger dinners. He does the same thing, vice versa. They don't love each other when they're pissed off, and they don't hate each other when they have sex."

"I don't think most of us are that clear-cut. My ex-

Sam D'Allesandro

lover and I always talked. About everything. It always left me sort of uncatharted. I mean it's just too hard to be adult and practical about everything all the time. Something gets missed. I need something a little violent once in a while. Rough sex doesn't always do the trick."

"Right. Eat too much and you get sicker. It's just like I'm saying: I want something more bestial; I want to run naked with snarling dogs in the park. You know, the brotherly bite, power of the pack, all that stuff."

"Hmm. I'm not so sure. Primitivism may be fine for artists, but you can't live off of it. I mean wake up and smell the coffee, you try running around naked in the park all night and you'll freeze, coming home at 4 a.m. with a stupid look on your face, a cold ass, shriveled balls, and dog shit on your feet. That is if someone doesn't catch you out there first, cut your head off, and seal you up in a fifty-five-gallon drum. It happens. Just last year."

When I think about this conversation, I can only recall with effort which speaker was Sid and which was me. We never think exactly the same way about anything at the same time. Then the next week we change positions and take the opposite side. Things are never black and white for us. From the very beginning we've always worked better in the gray zones.

Sid taking one last stab at an increasingly nebulous subject: "Maybe what I mean is I want to either win big in life or else get put down in a big way. I need something big. I'm willing to take a chance. Why not, right?"

Once, in the beginning, I started to make love to Sid in the middle of the night thinking he was Farrell. I was dreaming that Sid's body was Farrell's body, down to the last detail. I was going crazy, kissing him, running my hands up and down him, when I suddenly realized it was Sid and froze. I couldn't go on, the shock was too devastating. Like I'd just been punched in the stomach. I

112

The Wild Creatures

pretended to drop off to sleep again.

I'm telling you about Sid because he's the opposite of Farrell. Sid and I have had this plan for a year to hit every low-life neighborhood cocktail lounge in the city. I've got a list: three down, twenty-three to go. We keep going back to the same three. Last night was our seventh or eighth trip to The Zombie Pit. So far, no matter what we've done, they've never thrown us out.

The other two places we like to go are The Buddha Bar in Chinatown and The Persian Aub Zam Zam. We always get thrown out but have fun seeing just how insignificant an abrasion of the rules will be required. Usually all nonregulars get tossed in less than fifteen minutes. Since we're now up to about twenty-thirty minutes at The Buddha Bar, I think we may be on the way to being considered regulars someday. Then the biggest part of the fun will be over. Still, there will always be something deliciously mysterious and smarmy about having a Tsingtao beer beneath a giant gold Buddha lit with red candles.

Tonight our friend Dorrie comes along. She picks the bar. So far, tonight is the sleaziest I've ever seen in this town. I try not to touch anything. The place smells — if you shut your eyes, we could be in a South American marketplace at the end of a hot day. We're sitting at a table in the back trying to look invisible. I don't know why we're still here except that Sid has half a beer left. On the way here, Dorrie said, "You'll love this place." I don't know why I take the word of someone who works in a massage parlor that lures in Japanese businessmen with promises of sex and then offers no sex and very little massage. At dinner the other night, she told a story about riding one of her clients like a horse down the hall to the bathroom where she made him drink out of the toilet. I can't help wondering if that's what he thought he was paying for when he went in. "I'm so glad I found massage after that string of crummy jobs. It's just perfect

113

Sam D'Allesandro

for me." With that she smiles as serenely as an angel and reapplies startling red lipstick.

A young Latino guy who's been dancing over by the jukebox is now up on top of the bar, the glasses and used napkins that no one's bothered to pick up shoved to one side. I'm waiting for one of those little kicks he does to send a lipstick-coated beer bottle flying into someone's face. When he peels off his shirt (I thought it was a straitjacket), his chest appears to be bigger naked than clothed. "How could that thin layer of cotton have held all that in?" He's showing off a torso so tight it looks like you could pop the whole thing with a pin. The thought makes me nauseous. As I take another sip of Sid's beer the pants come off. He's wearing an aqua blue jockstrap beneath, one size too small, the first rows of public hair curling out the top. The ass is tan and smooth. I wonder if he shaves it.

Dorrie and Sid love this stuff. Somehow I can't really get involved anymore. The guy rotates his hips around in an ever-widening arc, over and over, his whole body making a complete turn on the little bar every few seconds. He's like a pirouetting ballet star on speed. Each complete turn tilts the head back, as if the rest of the body can only make its revolution in response to the tilt. The way he does it looks innate: tilt your head back at that angle and you whirl. I try it in my chair but it doesn't quite seem to work. Anyway I'm starting to think about leaving. My attention's starting to drift after about ten minutes of watching him execute this same move over and over. I decide it's all designed to show off his navel and flat, brown belly, ricocheting off the broad hips like a Mad Mouse roller coaster about to go off the track.

"See that guy on the bar?" says Sid. "That's Little Ricky, he does this all the time. This part's nothing, he's just warming up. Pretty soon he'll be letting these old men stick quarters in his asshole." A moment later I take

114

The Wild Creatures

my eyes off of Sid long enough to focus on the bar. Little Ricky's maneuvering his ass toward someone, somehow managing to tame his gyrating hips just long enough to hold steady while the man spots his exact target and with a shaking hand pushes something inside. It looks like a dime. Of course, I have no way to be sure since it's gone now.

"That looked like a dime," I say to Sid, trying to sound casual while actually shocked.

"That was a dime. He starts out with dimes and then advances up to quarters later on. Every once in a while he goes in the back room behind the bar and empties out."

I lean back in my chair as far as it will go without crashing to the floor, wondering if the thin legs might break. I've had enough of this place. Leaning still a dangerous inch further, what I'm really trying to do is get away. Distancing. I take possession of the rest of Sid's beer. He and Dorrie are only three feet away. That's enough to make them inaudible to me over the blaring disco music. That's enough to make them across the room.

As Little Ricky continues his human piggy bank routine, I'm thinking about the act that was on when we first arrived. It's like a nightmare I can't get out of my head. An overweight woman with pasty skin, the kind that looks like you could put your finger right through if you touched her, like Muenster cheese, did a routine with fruit and vegetables. She'd place an item between her large breasts, demonstrate how it could stay by itself, do a little dance involving various shimmying moves (as if daring the piece of fruit to try and get away), and then offer a patron the chance to snare one of the edibles by mouth. Soon various men and one woman are smeared with juices dripping from their chins. Smashed bananas, peach pulp, cantaloupe seeds.

She suddenly abandons the bar, dancing across the

wobbly tabletops until she's standing on mine. Her fleshy figure looms above me. I shrink backward until I'm trapped against the wall behind me. I try to scream but nothing comes out. I'm afraid to look up, but I can hear her laughing above me, placing one sharp high heel against my chest. Bending menacingly toward me, her swaying chest aims at my head and in one swift maneuver entraps my face between the two enormous balloons of warm, sticky flesh. I'm suffocating, literally, my mouth and nostrils filled with her expanding skin and the remains of a cantaloupe. Using only her breasts, she shakes my head viciously from side to side, in the same way a dog kills a small rodent, until my neck snaps and I finally slump from my chair to the floor.

So this is the real entertainment. This is Sid's betrayal. I've unwittingly fallen upon a snuff bar in which I've ended up the night's main attraction. I should have known.

When I come to, Little Ricky's up to quarters. Sid tells me he's already disappeared a few times to empty out. I guess I missed that part. I've begun to develop an elaborate fantasy about the woman with the fruit in which she's an everyday New Jersey housewife who just does this two nights a week for a little exercise and pocket money. At home in a cotton dress, in an overly sunny house painted white inside and out, she's as prim and perky as Donna Reed.

"Juicing oranges for the kids before sending them off to school," Sid adds.

I think the problem keeping us from the other twenty-three neighborhood cocktail lounges on our list is that we don't like drinking that much anymore. As soon as I'm past the drinking part and into the just plain drunk part I always think I'd rather be either fattening up my cortex some more with late-night TV, or else drinking espresso with Sid until we're both completely

The Wild Creatures

wired. We drink a lot of it, then right when we get to that edge where our eyes are popping and our brains will explode if we have one more pot, we have it and we're over the top: speeding up until we're both doing simultaneous monologues careening into a verbal hand-gesturing car crash 90 mph on a twisting turning psychic mountain pass, noise screeching, wind of our own voices cyclonic, everything on the little dinette table a blur and whaaaaam...we end up on the kitchen floor laughing hysterically with the chairs on top of us. It's always simultaneous. We lie on the linoleum and have a cigarette. Then we either go to bed or else one of us goes home, depending on whose place we're at.

Of course things aren't always that symbiotic. At one point I had this to say to Sid: "I don't think you ever really wanted me. You just needed someone around to bounce off of. Sort of like Ricky Ricardo was for Lucy, until she dumped him."

SID: "I'd say it was the other way around. You think you can do anything, anything, and it will never be going too far because I'll keep things from blowing up completely: make sure you get home on bad nights, make sure the rent gets paid, make sure the apartment doesn't burn down, make sure you don't accidentally kill yourself. Of course, I never really stop you from doing anything. My job is to watch. That's what you need, not someone to be with, just someone to watch you."

ME: "Come on, you're sitting on the sidelines watching me? The real problem's you can't stop your own out-of-control propulsion long enough to take me into much consideration. You want whatever you want to be enough for me. You think I should just sit back and enjoy the design you have for our lives, easy. You've got the hard part, coming up with all the ideas, new things to entertain us, go here, go there. Well, it's not enough. There's another person involved here, you know. Me.

117

Sam D'Allesandro

Let's face it, you don't want a lover, you just want a sidekick. Someone new to tell your history to."

Apparently there was a growing list of things that he was pretty sick of. After he told me that he didn't want to have sex with me anymore and then showed up begging for it two days later; after he told me I was projecting my well-deserved self-deprecation on him every time I voiced a petty observation only meant for his own self-improvement; after he told me I wasn't being straight with him when I once replied to a loaded inquiry, "You act like you're talking to someone who gives a shit," I had to say: "Come on, do you really think I'd bother to pretend I didn't care if I did? Do you really think I would perform for you just to get your attention?"

Actually I would. I care that much about Sid. I care because he doesn't...enough. In the beginning, I wanted to not care too much, to allow him to just entertain me. Now I care a lot. If he's decided to want me, I want him to want me nonstop. I want him to want me until he's completely drenched with me, saturated with my mannerisms—the cute ones, the gross ones, the ones that start out cute until you've seen them so many times they become gross—until he's disgusted with his inability to live life any way but vicariously, through me, until he finds me so perfect in the arty mess of the shortcomings and unrealized potential smeared across my apartment, until he wants to be me so much, while simultaneously being so horrified of the thought, that he'll have to kill me just to put a stop to the nightmare. I want to be that queasy feeling in the pit of his stomach. The subject of his novel, the hard-on, the sexual anxiety, the neurotic obsession, the vertigo and salmonella and impetigo of a lifetime. Like some kind of dirt under his fingernails that's driving him crazy and will never come out.

If he really wanted me, it would be like that. Then I

would know I was loved. Then I would think he really cared.

ME: "Listen, don't talk to me about who started what. You're the one who accused me of being from another planet and inhabiting an innocent boy's body. I don't mind the statement, it's the accusation part that gets me, the tone—like what you meant when you said it is that you think there's something wrong with me. Maybe there is, but I'm not sure I need to hear it all the time. Don't you understand? I am from another planet, one you've never been to. I thought you probably knew that."

SID: "I think you know what the truth is. All I'm saying is I need more attention right now. Sometimes all you do is take. I can't seem to fill you up."

ME: "It's hard not to take when I need so many things I'm not getting. Listening to your complaints, I feel like I have to be very careful what I reveal to you and how I reveal it, like balancing a pin on the surface of a glass of water. I'm neurotic in a different way than that. You should know that by now."

SID: "I don't want you to feel like you have to be careful, but you also can't go around just dropping these little bombs about what's wrong with us and then run away."

ME: "I'm not sure that running away when a bomb's dropped is an inappropriate response. I can't always answer everything you ask. Sometimes you can learn a lot about someone through some small hints about the past you never could have gotten if the complete historical film had rolled instead. Maybe I shouldn't say anything, you're right, because it's true I'm not always ready to say everything...but what's not responded to is meaningful too. By the way, I dreamt about you last night."

SID: "Don't be coy. Let's face it, I want love, you want

119

Sam D'Allesandro

to be left alone."

ME: "First, don't expect me to rise in anger and clarify if you're going to use provocation as a ploy. Second, I don't have time to be coy. The truth is, it doesn't come that unpracticed to me."

(With that, I suddenly realize that I've somehow bitten off more than I would like to chew at the moment. I've always hated the phrase "Don't dish it out if you can't take it" because I've always been so much better at dishing it out. I move to escape.)

"Actually I dreamt you had two sets of eyebrows. I thought they were pretty sexy." Then I tell Sid about the rest of the dream. We're in a motorboat speeding along on a lake. Sid's driving, steering from the back of the boat with a lever that comes out of the engine. I'm in the front. My half of the boat sinks several feet and then continues to move forward at this new level, under-water. The water comes just to my forehead. My life jacket holds me to my seat and I can't move to save myself. I'm beginning to drown. Only the front of the boat is underwater, Sid's half is still fine. I wonder if he's noticed what's happening and will save me.

A friend told me about walking home one night and finding torn-out pages from boy magazines, one by one, strewn in his path all the way to his house. He followed them like bread crumbs. One of those pages could have been Farrell. I have a magazine like that, with a picture of him two or three years older than when I knew him. That's the magazine I masturbated over this morning. That's the picture I accidentally ruined.

I can't help wondering about the significance. The only time Farrell tells me he loves me comes in the middle of postvomiting waves of nausea. I'm four years younger. It's 4 a.m. Still hot. The car is stopped in a deadly quiet New Orleans neighborhood. No dogs, no crickets, no drunks. We're on our way home from a

The Wild Creatures

goodbye crawfish feed. We are the ones being said goodbye to, tomorrow we leave for Los Angeles, pulling a U-Haul with a car that's barely been making it around town as it is. When I cut the lights, I find there's enough moon to throw shadows.

Farrell is shirtless, on hands and knees in the grass, eyes rolling. The body's beautiful even while convulsing. The vomit smells only of the salty crawfish brine and red wine that caused it—almost sweet. Burgundy-hued in the warm air. "I love you" comes when he's resettled and slouched in the car seat, near a pass-out he'll never quite hit. His eyes are closed. For the first moment I only look at him and wonder if he meant it. In the second moment, I'm wondering if he even said it, if I ever heard it.

I start the engine and the car rolls off down the road. My hands are steering but my mind is so far away that I can't recall the ground just covered. It's a small shock when we actually reach the little house on St. Phillip. We lie down for two hours before both waking up hungover and unable to sleep. We load the car, leaving behind a huge pile of stuff on the curb that won't fit, and drive off toward Texas. Toward Los Angeles.

In the bar, the very first night, I can't stop looking at him, the deep chestnut hair, the perfect body, the fine features beneath the scars that draw me so completely. It's as if I can smell his scent from across the room. From the very beginning, he's something wild for me.

The markings that track his face are the only distraction from something otherwise classically pure in every way. They're the uniqueness that makes him perfect for me. Alive. Not just a wonderful doll manufactured by a brilliant artist working with only my desires in mind. More. Better. They provide a rawness, a sexual charge to what would otherwise be only extraordinarily handsome. I look around. That's when I realize for the

Sam D'Allesandro

first time that others are repelled by beauty in such an agonized state.

We're sitting on a gray high-tech couch listening to a Blue Angels tape I've never heard before. He stops talking, as if suddenly realizing the unnecessity, and kisses me. The kiss doesn't stop until my pants, shirt, and watch have been removed, until I'm led into the bedroom, onto the bed, and enveloped beneath a sheet of warm skin.

His body is the most beautiful. Since I clearly can't get enough of it, he feels safe in asking if I'd like to rub it down with baby oil. After I do, in the middle of the part that follows, both of us are drenched with sweat, at the point when the highest pinnacle has been reached but still our lips won't unlock—perhaps another peak could follow, as high or higher—in the middle of that part I reach up to touch his face. I know it's too personal a move but I can't help it. I'm drawn. The animal inside of me supersedes and the touch becomes inevitable. I have to, to verify the texture. To make sure it's real.

He smoothly and firmly removes my hands and holds my arms against the bed. Then he resumes kissing me.

His face is like a map: Xs and lines curve around the cheekbones in a constant motion of intersections and near-misses. Little seams round the earlobes from an operation. The skin is damaged with a deep and haphazard set of cuts I can only imagine coming from a violent moment. He doesn't talk about that. He never lets me touch them.

Two months later this happens: I pin his arms and holding him against the wall I kiss his face all over. "Let me," I say. He struggles but only vaguely. Instead a little whimper begins in his throat. His lips begin to kiss back at whatever part of my face they can reach. I move for the eyes, the curve of the mouth. I lick and probe every little trench and ridge and rent. Every movement my

122

The Wild Creatures

fingers have longed to trace. I've wanted to live in these scars, now I open the web and lie down inside, sucking out the invisible poison that's kept us apart. When he lets me do it, I dare to imagine for the first time that he might love me.

Driving across the Southwest, my head in his lap, I watch headlights slowly swerve through the car's interior in a rhythm. One at a time. In Texas, my turn driving, I spill coffee all over myself when I brake for a jerk in a Galaxie 500 reaching into his backseat to slap one of his kids. Farrell can't stop laughing and I get mad. Later that night we sleep pulled over on the side of a back road. Farrell leans against the car door with his long legs stretched out on the seat. I sit between his legs and lie against him. It's his idea. We sleep this way all night. I can hear his heart beat and feel the heat of his skin. The moment is so tender and bound to pass, that I'm nearly in tears.

I have an image of him at about eight or nine in a sunny, green, flower-filled meadow. He's already handsome. His chestnut hair is shining. His skin is smooth. His vision is a blur of color — it's so beautiful out that his eyes don't need to focus, the picture's the same intensity, fuzzy as it is sharp. Maybe more so fuzzy. He has no need for sharpness yet. He's eight or nine and has no feelings of sadness, despair, or shame. No experience of being an outsider. The sun is shining, the meadow green and flowered, the boy nearly perfect.

Ten years later a different Farrell walks down a dark and narrow New Orleans street. It's late. The street seems empty, but here and there a man can be spotted leaning against a doorframe, seemingly doing nothing. One of these is waiting for Farrell, will want to take him off this street and into a bed. One of these will want to touch him all night for one night, and then disappear. He may even leave money, or if he's ugly he may offer money to begin with. At this hour, on this dark street, most

Sam D'Allesandro

of those present will want Farrell and will overlook the part of him they don't like to get to the part they do. Farrell decides which he wants. He doesn't care about the money, but if it comes he'll take it. There's an excitement in that for him that he accepts but doesn't quite understand. None of these men who want him tonight will take him out to dinner, become his friend, or be seen with him in public again. He embarrasses them with his perfect face in ruins. They want him only in their bed. That means outside of their bed they don't want him.

I had this idea I could protect him. Keep him from being hurt. I figured he must need that. Actually it turns out to be exactly the part he can't take. He's learned to live without protection. He's convinced that he wants the men he picks up to disappear by morning. I'm one of a very few to ever be different. From the beginning, I tell myself his love was confirmed in that small way. It's part of my evidence that it existed.

Everything will change when we get to Los Angeles. I already know that as I'm packing the car, as I'm kissing him for the last time in the now-empty house on St. Phillip, as I'm sleeping against his chest on the quiet back road in Texas. We're about to exit the peacefully static territory between leaving here and arriving somewhere else. L.A. is Farrell's new start — I was never part of that plan. Love was never supposed to creep into this deal.

In L.A., we take a drug and Farrell wears my red tennis shoes to Studio One. The place is packed but we don't see anyone else the whole night. The next day, on Venice Beach, he tells me about the scars.

His hands absentmindedly grab up little fistfuls of the beige California sand, and then let them go again. The sky's a deep blue, a hundred times bluer than the white-gray days that pass for clear in California. A blue

124

The Wild Creatures

like the sky in my picture of Farrell as a boy. He's lying on his stomach, propped up on his elbows to create a perfect curve from his neck to his ass. A Speedo makes a tiny ridge against the tan skin. My eyes do a smooth and careful sweep, reconfirming what they already know, and return to the face. They fall into a deep line, in a swift diagonal, back over to the sudden conclusion of mouth—settling intently on the slow-moving lips. The lips are calmly reporting blood, violence, disaster, and pain in a soft monotone.

I want to tell him he doesn't have to tell me. He says he knows that, he wants to. He's been wondering when I would ask. I want to say I never would have, but since I really don't know that I say nothing.

A month later at LAX, Farrell cries as he hugs me goodbye in a crowded airport waiting area.

I have a recurring dream. In it I'm chasing Farrell across barren, fog-shrouded hills. The grass is an icy glass crunching beneath me, making little cuts in the leather soles of my boots. Farrell is getting smaller and smaller, farther and farther away. Sensation sinks in slowly, it's colder, the icy grass turns to snow. I look down to find my bare feet leaving tracks of blood against the white.

Then I'm back in my bed and realizing it was just a dream. Farrell's face appears over my bed, hovering, staring sweetly. I try to reach up to him. I'm nailed to the ground, the bed's disappeared. Each of my hands is marked with a big scrawly X. Above me, Farrell's face begins to thin, like smoke, getting fainter. I pull harder against the nails, my skin gives a little but I still can't get up. His voice is saying something about motion that I can't quite get, over and over, as his image breaks up and he disappears.

I'm starting another pot of espresso on the stove. I'm thinking about how I used to imagine certain people out of my past that I'm no longer in contact with, watching me through a crystal ball or some sort of telepathic power I never knew they had. They'd be seeing everything: me being cooler than I used to be when they knew me, me tripping over the curb, me in particularly mortifying masturbation sequences (but doesn't everybody have those?), everything. I wonder if Farrell can do that and if he's doing it right now. There's a little animal inside of me. It's helped me to understand that a lot of things you wouldn't think could really happen, do.

Like the being-made-invisible thing. I hate the way you have to fight to keep from being made invisible all the time. On the street sometimes people walk right through me. At parties I speak and the person I'm talking to doesn't hear my voice, launching into their own story while I'm in midsentence. I hate the not-hearing of my words when it's clear that the person's not deaf but more like pretending my voice carries no volume. Not low volume, no volume.

It's as if I'm just a mouth moving soundlessly in graceful dips and circles and rat-a-tat-tats. The teeth occasionally flash; lips press together in a sexual motion, dissolve into each other, quickly part, and then repeat in a series of convulsive jerks; coyly the tongue uncoils, begging release from between the prison of teeth before retreating into the dull cave of throat; little swirls and sparkles of sweet and embarrassingly untrained saliva manifest and pop, and all the while dark air funnels out in columns like smoke, to hover a moment before dissipating. All without sound.

That's what people do to me. As if I wasn't there. As if I'm some escaped idea that accidentally fell out of someone. Someone who has voice, has visibility, has embodiment. All the things I seem to lack. It's as if I fell out of someone's head and was forgotten and left behind. Sometimes I just sit and watch when it happens, wondering about the mechanics of feeling real while

The Wild Creatures

having no real form to others. Like a little story where only I can see what's happening.

It's not that I wouldn't love to be able to become invisible — that could certainly have some advantages. It's just that I don't want other people making me that way at all sorts of odd moments. The way Farrell did. That makes me have to remind myself that Sid doesn't. In a world of people looking through me, putting their hands right in me as if there were no barrier of skin between us, a world with a permanent image of parties where others take my volume away — all as if I wasn't really there — Sid looks at me. Sid listens to me. In spite of almost continuous conflict, he's becoming like a warm hallucination. Like just what I've needed for a long time. I know it sounds corny. It's just that I was so glad when he told me he didn't hate me and didn't just want to fuck me.

There's a baby named Sperm on the night table in my bedroom that Sid and I made together. He's locked inside of an oblong glass bottle that's sealed at both ends. Inside he bubbles around all day. He's just molecules and he'll never be anything more. It's perfect. He'll always be happy this way. I love to watch him. He's mostly reddish-pink, no little veins or features or anything, beyond embryonic, nothing to mess up his total basicness, his incredible cellularness, his intense display of sheer unconscious animation, suspended in golden fluid. He will never die, and he can't get away from me the way Farrell did. Long after Sid's gone, he'll still be here. Now I've told you another one of my secret parts.

Last night I dreamed there was a five-color map of the United States tattooed on my belly, just below the navel, Maine reaching up around the left-hand side. I can't remember how and when the map got there. Nothing comes to mind, no sleazy tattoo parlor, no drunken sex

Sam D'Allesandro

partner with a pin and lots of colorful ink against the gray background of a tiny jail cell, no Arabian adventure with a modern twist. I can't remember if it hurt to have it put on or if it would hurt to have it taken off.

This dream reminds me of how I wish I could sink into my dreams and find a way to live there. The way I'm drifting through my life right now makes me think I'd rather be doing that in a dream instead, where things are more interesting and an observer can really feel something new is always happening. Fly, jump fifty feet, go around the world. Be invisible.

There's a little animal inside of me. It has different names at different times and sometimes it has no name. Sometimes I think it's made up of equal parts of Farrell, my mother, and LSD. Sid and I are its victims.

There's a little animal inside of me. It's eating me. It's building me each day. It starts with a blank lump and animates the person it wants from it. It controls me. It makes me do things. It won't let me stop thinking about it. Other times I can't think at all and I become more like a small fire emitting a lot of sparks that pass for talking, sex, behavior. A walking zombie pit where anything can fall into me.

If the animal inside's not sleepy, it doesn't let me sleep. It tends to manufacture more mental violence than I can contain. Sometimes at night I'll be lying in bed, almost asleep, everything almost right, and then it comes. It makes me start thinking about all sorts of terrible things and then I can't stop thinking about them. Like what if I fall asleep and when I wake up I find out I've killed someone? Or what if I wake up and can't open my eyes? What if the next time I answer the phone a wire short-circuits and sends a deadly wave of electricity shooting through my brain, only I don't die and turn into a vegetable for the rest of my life? Or what if the next time I take a shower glass comes out instead of water and cuts me into little tiny pieces and then Sid comes in

The Wild Creatures

and doesn't see me there in the bottom of the tub and washes me down the drain? What if I fall onto the subway's electrified third rail during a drug flashback, or I wake up and everyone else in the world is dead, or I'm in a crowded department store and suddenly realize I'm naked, or my building moves while I'm at work and I can never find it again? What if my penis falls off or my fingers grow inside of my hands or my skin shrinks? I could be attacked in my own apartment by a rabid dog. The little kid down the street might finally brain me with his skateboard, beating me to death at the curb as all the other neighbors look on in a trance. What if I acquire a horrible smell and I'm never ever able to get rid of it and nobody wants to be my friend anymore? What if I wake up and I'm fourteen again and have to go through high school all over and everything that's happened so far has just been a crazy dream? Sometimes I lie there at night with these thoughts flashing through my mind. It's like a Ferris wheel in which each car contains a different little nightmare, spinning faster and faster. I'm on it and I can't get off.

The little animal inside does that. It's the thing that marks up my mind in the middle of the night. Marks it up into a messy smear. Until it's the Zombie Pit. If it were on paper, my first-grade teacher, Mrs. Farmer, would have ripped it to shreds in front of the entire terrified class. David Reynolds smirks in the front row. Mrs. Farmer retreats to her fourteenth cup of coffee in the teachers' lounge to bask in the glory of another humiliation skillfully executed.

I wake up and try to relax, meditate, forget about it, but a gigantic war between a mind riddled with neurotic impulses and enough residual Benzedrine to last three or four lifetimes breaks out and beats the meditative core of inner peace to a bloody, quivering pulp. I wake up and try to forget. I try to forget and go back to sleep; I try to forget and I can't.

Sam D'Allesandro

I wake up and remember. I sit upright in bed, sickened with a certainty that I've been a fool to believe Sid could love me. For a nightmarish moment, Mrs. Farmer's hideous face blends with a superimposed image of Farrell's scarred perfection. Then a transparent overlay of Sid appearing in his true form as a smirking David Reynolds sandwiches itself between the two. It's the devil, it's a pitiful Down's syndrome child in a state institution, it's a lover out for revenge, a ghost, a hunchback, a witch. It's Vanessa Redgrave leering and drooling in *The Devils* as she points the accusing finger that will send me to the stake.

It's a million things except the Farrell that held me when I woke up yelling in a strange hotel room, told me he loved me after he vomited crayfish, cried in a crowded airport waiting lounge while kissing me goodbye. He did all of those things. The little animal inside of me takes those moments and his beautiful scars and twists them into little sentences that say, "I never loved you." Stacked row upon row across Farrell's otherwise-smooth cheeks. Bending slightly as they round the high cheekbones. Now multiplying and shrinking simultaneously. Now so small it would take a magnifying glass to read them, like the tiny story etched into a Chinese ivory carving.

If I can't get inside of a better dream, then I need a womb. Or a father, one who lets me do whatever I want, but pays the bills and makes the hard decisions. Or a drug that never lets me down, or a good fuck—good enough to get lost in and stay right at that point where you totally lose control. Good enough to stay right there for at least six hours and then pass out. A new fuck, a new engine, a new purr, something to stop a clicking mind on the rampage. I need a better dream I need a womb I need a father I need a drug that doesn't let me down I need a fuck good enough to get lost in I need a triumph. Or maybe a good beating, because that's when

130

The Wild Creatures

the little animal inside of me would lose control, if I let someone else take over.

Then, when it gets me back, it will probably really make some turmoil to compensate for anything it's missed.

Now Sid's image wafts through my head. He looks like an angel. His face is so sweet it confuses me. Sid claims that upon meeting him I was a study in cool. Just the right stance and naked silence. Heating up the small room with my careless sexual nature. That's more or less what he reported. I remember the whole thing differently, but I'm working on switching my perception of the event to follow his storyline. I want to learn to paint myself in as good a light as he does.

I want to be very perfect within each given setting. ME: perfectly cool, uncaring yet fluidly conversational with the important/strange at the cocktail party where I know almost no one. ME: cocky and interesting in a captivating sort of way as I heat up the room with a careless sexual nature that slightly threatens and promises absolutely nothing. ME: perfectly in control of who will and will not even try to pick me up, and who will succeed. ME: strong and incredibly adaptable in every sexual situation, seizing just the cream of what's offered, devouring it, and tossing out the rest in a blameless manner. ME: doing everything, tirelessly, with all the pleasure and assuredness due my experience. Me smooth, me subtle, me roughly suave. Me making very good and carefully impulsive choices, forever. When I think about Sid's first impression, I can almost imagine being that person.

And he likes the little animal inside. According to Sid, I should admit that life really only comes out amusing when "I allow" the animal to get me whipped up. When it acts like my brain's on fire, things really get hysterical. Sid says I should give it credit for that. Of course he doesn't exactly understand the animal or he wouldn't have thrown in that "I allow" part, but he has the general picture. After all, he lives with it.

With Sid's view in mind, I've been trying to learn to be more cheerful. He's helping me, just a little, to become friends with the animal. To think of it as part of me rather than just the powerful psychic parasite that it is. And that's basically the same thing Ed was saying over coffee at Corbas: like it or not, this is living. Of course I prefer to put it a different way: the tongue's on the wall and I think I've been swallowed.

It's basically the same viewpoint. So I've decided to admit that I'm not yet rich nor egregiously hirsute, just two of the things I thought I might have wanted to be by now. And I'm ready to admit that sleeping next to a befurred Sid is as close as I'm going to get to Farrell. Maybe that's enough. In fact I will never be egregiously hirsute. Sid is instead. I'm not living in an L.A. barrio on a warm night watching Farrell's gorgeous sleep. I'm not getting closer to the goal of visiting all twenty-six local dives on the list with Sid, the one I want to love but will never love as much as I loved Farrell.

But the bars on the list are really my goal. Sid's goal, from our first moments together, has been to try and get me to drop out of my head and into the world. Because that's where he is.

At the turn of the century, the average age of death for the American male was 46.2 years, 48.3 for women. Sid would have eleven years to go. Farrell would have had sixteen. Now we're up to 69.2 years for males and 76.9 for females. That would give both Sid and Farrell considerably more time left. My first lover died when she was twenty-three and already a mother. My mother died when she was thirty-two. Farrell disappeared when he was thirty.

Now I've let you in on a few more of my secret parts. I'm walking along a wide, steamy beach. Cold water,

The Wild Creatures

close by and hazardous. The colors of my tattooed "United States" are dim and graying in the thin light. Sid's busy telling me about the girl in the aqua miniskirt getting him kicked out of the Pyramid Club the night before, as if it had happened just the night before.

We find a wedding dress, wet and tangled in a pile near the surf. Sid takes off his clothes and puts it on. His skin is red and mottled from the cold irritation of the sandy, clammy garment. It's long, used to be longer, with little rips along the bottom. It's beautiful and torn and forlorn. It's filthy and ruined and drags along the wet sand in back. I picture an Italian girl with long black hair stopping her slow walk to remove the dress, letting it fall in a pile in the shallow waves before walking off naked down the shore. In the dark mist her skin is cold, but she doesn't notice. Her hair is wet and salty, her gaze set on the distance. Feet move slowly, gracefully, knowingly, one after the other.

Travels with My Mother

[*Tape begins.*] I'm thinking about a film Coco was in. In it, he walks the entire length of a warehouse-turned-theater with his friend Lulu, chatting all the way. He's wearing his fake leopard-skin jacket, a lot of makeup, his thick, damaged black hair tied up in a bun. He's talking about a sailor he met the night before. "At least he *said* he's a sailor; I got a hat and three hundred dollars." His stream of consciousness conversation, although largely meaningless, is amazing to listen to. The last thing I remember him doing is turning to Lulu and saying, "And that's why you're my best girlfriend."

The last time I saw Coco was at a gallery opening. It was about midnight when he walked in, again in a leopard-skin coat, and made his way to the food table, by now decimated and empty. There was a platter with some lettuce and tomatoes that had served as a bed for whatever it was that had sat on top of it, and he began eating the lettuce and the tomatoes, really the only scrap of food left on the table. That was about midnight: by four he would be dead. They found him on Divisadero Street, on the sidewalk, one arm out of his leopard-skin coat, another tooth knocked out, and now crusting on the sidewalk in a tiny pool of vomit. It was a heroin overdose, and I'm thinking about that now, I guess because I recently resaw this film, as I drive toward my parents, four hours away.

My mother and father are divorced now. I'll stay at my mother's for a few days, and then we're thinking of taking a trip together, a small trip, a drive in her RV. I need to get away for a while, and she likes the company. There's nothing that needs to be done when I'm there. We have breakfast, mandatory no matter how late you stay up the night before, and that's it. No lunch, though

134

The Wild Creatures

there's food in the refrigerator. The rest of the day is spent in walks for me, sitting down in the lawn chairs in the backyard for her, talking to whoever will come and sit with her. There's no real work to be done.

It's different with my father. He lives in the city now. Visiting him is full of going to steak houses and helping out with little projects around the house. The projects he wants me to help him with now he doesn't really need my help on. In fact, a lot of the time I end up sitting and watching him because it's not something I can really help with, like fixing a dishwasher. I hand him a wrench every once in a while. It's unlike the list he used to keep for me on the refrigerator door when I was growing up. That list contained more important things, things needing to be done on the small ranch: rewiring fences, fixing the hay crib, things like that. For three summers in a row I was supposed to pull star thistle out that grew up in the yard, for two hours a day. Star thistle grows about two feet tall, a tuft of hairy bloom surrounded by sharp spikes. If you didn't pull it all out of the yard every year, it would come back thicker. So I was out with my gloves, pulling away in the hundred-degree heat, running in for a break every twenty minutes and a glass of Kool-Aid, then running back out again. This, until I got a job in an orchard in town.

As I arrive at my mother's place, I notice the big heavy wooden gate, chained open, as usual. When I was growing up, this gate had to be opened and shut every time you went in or out. Usually one of us kids would drag the heavy gate on sagging hinges to the post, then lever it, lift it up enough to slide the bolt into the slot. Otherwise the cows and sheep would get out, ending up a mile away down the dirt road. I'd run down barefoot, with maybe my little brother, and try to herd them back in. Maybe my dad would show up in the car on his way back from work, and we'd all get on the car and herd them from there, my brother and I sitting on the hood of the car, clapping our hands as we went.

(Then you can have some caustic talk with your sister, maybe, at the ranch, and then...) I sleep in my old room, even though it's not really my room anymore, long since turned into my father's office before he moved out. But there's a fold-out couch in there, and my stereo's still here. My records are still in the closet. I sit down on the couch, put on blah blah blah. On the opposite wall are pictures of us kids as kids, and a big card I made for them in the second grade, that says blah blah blah. My eyes travel past the stereo to the sliding-glass window, and I stare out into the dark night. I can only see as far as this huge oak tree twenty feet away. Then the wooden slat fence not far beyond that. I grab my jacket and decide to go out for a while.

I end up sitting on the hood of my car, staring up at the stars. There seem to be a zillion of them. Perfectly white bright spots against a blanket of black, rather than the light gray that serves as night in the city. The cat comes up and sits on the hood with me, settling into my lap for warmth. It's not my cat, my old cat Caleb—it's a new cat. Caleb's long since dead, something that came as a shock to me when my parents told me. When he was older, claims my mother, he would only sleep curled around her head, curled around the top of her head, and in the middle of the night he'd put his little paws softly against her eyes. When she'd wake up, she'd have to remember to gently remove his paws before opening them.

Two days later my mother and I load the RV and head for Oregon. I drive. On the second day I have my first migraine headache ever. My mother tries every prescription pharmaceutical on me she can come up with. She brings a whole treasure chest of them with her, but nothing seems to work. The antidepressants she keeps to herself.

The Wild Creatures

So now she's driving and I'm sitting on the seat next to her, eyes closed, slumped against the seat. (Not very much conversation here. Then there's a part later on where it snows, going over the mountains. We're stuck behind a snowplow for two hours. When the snowplow manages finally to clear the way, we're the first car through. Snow is still falling heavy enough to cover the tracks of the plow. Mom: "It's just a blanket of white. It's so pure. Everything's so white, it's so pure." And then I don't know what I say. But it's a special moment for us. Snowflakes bounce and sit on the windshield, hit and sit on the windshield for a moment before blowing off or sliding to the bottom and melting. It's nighttime now. The snow looks like tiny blah blah blah in the car lights. We've still got a long way to go.) (Later my mom lies down on the seat and puts her head on my lap. It's warm, it's snowing, I'm listening to a country station on the radio, the only thing that comes in, my mother and I in the RV. And then at the very end, another story: My mom says something about, "I've always been proud of you, no matter what. You're different from your brothers and sisters, but I think you and I are closer. I've always been proud of you, your father too. I don't think you always realized that.")

One day in the RV, the next day my mother wears a pair of my underwear. She's run out and she's having her period. She still has those. After a while I carefully ask her how they fit, with a little smile on my face. She says, "Like a pair of bikini panties, but they'll do." The picture of my mother wearing my jockey shorts still amuses me, and I chuckle for a long time as we're driving along. In Oregon we hit all the sights along the way. There's a place called the Blowhole on the coast where water shoots up out of a cave to form a geyser. We've gone through the giant redwoods and the Mystery Spot where nothing is square, where gravity's defied. Agate Beach, and the place where monarch but-

137

terflies gather to breed. My mom likes to stop at the little souvenir stores along the way. She buys postcards and cheap novels. She reads so fast, she reads about one a night before she turns out the light, only sleeping about four or five hours a day, unlike me, it's more like nine. I, on the other hand, while feigning as though I'm stopping for her, am the one who ends up buying all the kitsch, the little snow machines with blah blah blah inside, the little men made out of seashells, and one of those little poodles whose head bobs up and down. It's wearing a raincoat and a rain hat. This is mist country, after all.

One day we stop at the Redwood Beach. There are no trees standing here, but this is the spot where the trees wash up on the beach, like whales, every year around this time. It's great for scavenging. Sometimes you can actually find a glass Japanese fishing pole in the sand. That's considered a real treasure, but I've never found one. My mom found one broken once.

We settle down in the sand for a picnic. We're playing the Willie Nelson tape now (then quote a line from Willie Nelson). It's my mother's choice, but I don't mind either. When it's finished, I put on Brian Eno. I know she likes that and it relaxes both of us. There are other things I could play, but I try to find something that I know she'll like. We're both trying to enjoy this trip, to be pleasant, to avoid some of the blowups that we had on family outings in the past. It's just she and I. It should be different that way. We're finding out.

So far it is. When we reach my grandmother's in Seattle, and fall down for the heavy night's sleep, my mom picks the guest room and I sleep in the RV. The next day we all have breakfast: Missouri biscuits and gravy only my grandmother makes us. Then she and my grandmother settle into lawn chairs for a long talk, with their coffee. I pull the hose out of the garage, attach it to the faucet, and uncoil it so I can wash the van. Sooty drips run down the windshield and the hood from all

138

The Wild Creatures

that clean snow that later picked up every particle of dirt that was in the air. By the time I finish and go back in the house, my mom's sitting at the dinette, drinking still another cup of coffee, while my grandmother makes brownies. Those are for me, I know. They're my favorite. "Sara Lee," she says. "That's the secret. That's the best mix there is."

Later in the day, my grandmother tries to talk me into staying home and watching the football game. She can never get it through her head that I hate organized sports. In the end, I don't relent and, out of boredom, end up going shopping with my mother and my grandmother. At La Pointe's, my mother ends up trying on a blah blah blah dress. I don't know why. It's not like her at all. She's usually in jeans and a sweatshirt. I think it must be somehow to please my grandmother.

I have tuberculosis, and I've had it for almost a year. My mother's known that for a long time. My sister says she babies me. My sister doesn't know the complications of the illness. We're hoping during our trip that I'll stay well, but my mother has assured me that she's prepared to take over all the driving, and that we'll even head immediately back if need be. My grandmother knows that, too. That's why the brownies. I've lost twenty pounds and she's trying to fatten me up.

After the dress shop, my grandmother insists on taking us to the Banana Split Shop. It's an enormous ice cream parlor (and then describe it, the little pink-and-white-striped leatherette tables, and the little chairs in pink colors). I think she knows that I don't really — well, I try not to eat sugar these days, because I'm borderline hypoglycemic. But it's something she used to do when I was visiting as a kid. It's her way of loving me. Later that day, my mother asks me about Crawford. She's never met Coco but when she was visiting one day, Crawford dropped by to borrow some records (and then go ahead and tell the story of Crawford).

Sam D'Allesandro

We pass a giant Paul Bunyan made out of redwood, maybe fifteen feet high. His clothes are painted — bright red for his shirt, blue for the pants, a garish orange for the face flesh tones. He's wearing a metal hardhat. I'm not sure they really had metal hardhats at the time of Paul Bunyan, but here he does. There's no Babe the Blue Ox. But inside the wood-slat souvenir shop, *there* are Babe the Blue Oxes, made of redwood, standing glued to little tiny burls that say "Welcome to the Redwoods" on them. I end up buying a tiny redwood figure, just a ball for the head, a ball for the body, and sticks for the legs and arms, wearing a little hula skirt, big, big wide eyes, standing on a redwood burl next to a painted palm tree. When I show my mother and put it on the dash of the cab, she shakes her head and says, "Oh, honestly." (Then later describe, when you're talking about the migraine headache, how two Codeine 4s and a Valium 10 do the trick. It sent me floating. Half the time I could take in the scenery, and the other half my mind would be off somewhere else.)

While my mother and I were still thinking over the possibility of the trip, my sister Judith said, "What's the big deal, just go!" Judith who could spend the entire time talking about her house, her kids, a new pattern for her curtains, everything safe. My mother would enjoy that, too. But we're more intimate. Things come out. For a moment, I picture a teary, hysterical revelation in the cab of the truck about her final breakup with my father, even though it would be much likelier for her to give me this information calmly. Or, my illness could come up. We'd both come to grips with it, but it'd still cause my mother a lot of pain. I knew that she was worried about me. Her father had died of what I was sick with now. As Judith stared, waiting for a reply, my mother calmly took a sip of beer, looked her in the eyes and said, "Well, we're thinking about it. I'm not sure if I want to be gone that long or not."

The Wild Creatures

(Then later, in the RV, when we're driving along, let Mom give a few little details about the breakup with my father. She lets things slip about it, in small ways. A little piece of information here, a little piece of information there. Clues. When I ask her if she thinks she might ever remarry, she says, "Oh, I don't know. I've never really met anyone I liked as much as your father. And I decided I'd rather be alone than be with him. I like being alone, out on the ranch, having my coffee in the morning, taking walks. When I come home from work, it's quiet, and I can do whatever I want. I'm getting spoiled, you know?" My father had put it differently. The phone rang at about eleven o'clock. I've just come in from blah blah blah. "Your mother," he said, "has had what I think is a tiny nervous breakdown." "What do you mean?" "She asked for a divorce," my dad said. "I told her, 'You don't want a divorce. We'll work this out, we always have.' She said, 'I just want to be alone.' I can't understand it. It's been twenty-five years." "But sometimes," I said, "sometimes things change, Dad." "Umm," he said. "Umm, I think you should go up and see her, as soon as you can get away. I can't get a word out of her anymore. I want you to make sure she's okay." That weekend I spent with my mother revealed none of the hysterics my father had so prominently mentioned. She seemed very clear. She calmly told me in one breath, "I know what I want, I know you're here because you're worried about me, I just don't want to be married anymore, I want to spend time alone, I want some peace and quiet. Your father and I have changed. I end up yelling at him when he asks me too many questions, really only because I want it to be quiet. I want to sit quiet by myself. Then I feel guilty afterward. He doesn't understand. I think it's better this way." What she said all seemed reasonable to me. I didn't see any problem. So I avoided my two sisters' six-month flurry of continuous calls, their worrying about the situation.)

Sam D'Allesandro

I remember when I was fifteen and this room was still my bedroom, my mother bursting in one morning in her white terry-cloth bathrobe, just out of the shower, to tell me she'd just heard on the radio that Janis Joplin had overdosed on heroin. I was still in bed, not yet up, not yet getting ready for school. I couldn't believe it. I still played the *Kozmic Blues* album almost every morning while getting ready, after a previous long period of playing *Cheap Thrills* every morning while getting ready (this was before *Pearl*). My mother made her announcement very seriously. She knew it was important to me. It was my father that might have made some crack about "hippies and drugs" at the breakfast table. (You might use some other little stories taken from the trilogy poems, just, you know, that you're remembering when you're up at your mom's house—oh, and maybe mention Coco's bad habits—the hexes, the boiling eggs, the long-distance calls, and say how you would say, "Hello, how are you?" on the street but how it was dangerous to really let him think you were available. Maybe when Mom asks, "How's Crawford?" you might, I don't know, want to make that a really short thing, like just several sentences, like don't tell her how Crawford died at a party, she passed out and broke her nose, blah blah blah. You might want to just allude more to your disillusionment with the city without making it so much a part of the story.)

(In the part where Mom's sitting in the lawn chairs— my sister Judith will be there for the weekend before we go. She'll make sure that nothing difficult comes up, smoothing over any situation with a few sentences. Later that day, when my other sister accidentally mentions my father, Judith moves quickly to point out an ordinary antic that we've all seen a million times that one of her children is doing nearby. My mother looks at me with a little sidelong glance and rolls her eyes enough just for me to tell we both know what she's doing. The glance is

The Wild Creatures

to tell me that talking about my father wouldn't have bothered her.)

On the way out of CNA, Coco winks at me. His smile, with its missing front tooth, reminiscent of an Okie hillbilly; his hair tied up in a bun, as usual. He could almost be Minnie Pearl.

(Before we go on the trip, while my sisters are still there, you might do this: To the supermarket, to pick up some stuff for dinner. It's ten miles to town, but she's used to the drive, so am I. And then you could describe, I don't know, the automatic doors at the supermarket, how cold it is, the frozen-food section, what your mom buys, the trash magazines at the checkout counter, or the checkout woman herself, who could be a sort of caricature of small town places.)

Other places my mom and I pass on our trip: an enormous rock on the ocean that looks like a dinosaur, that we do stop and look at; Santa's Village (describe, with little candy canes for fence posts, maybe a big Santa's face where the front gate is the mouth), where we don't stop. I want to, but my mom says she's not in the mood, so I don't press it. If I pressed it, I know she'd give in, but I don't want to go that much.

(About my father in the city — if you open a window in the bathroom of his condo, the building next door is so close you feel you can almost reach out and touch it. He likes sushi now. At the end of the last time I visited him, just before Christmas last year, he introduced me to a woman he'd met and we all went out to dinner together. He didn't actually introduce her as his girlfriend, but I think he wanted me to get used to the possibility.)

A little later, the story comes up for the thousandth time about when my mother tried to explain the facts of life to me. My sisters love this story. It sends them into rolls of laughter no matter how many times they hear it. The way it goes is that my mother was reading one of her medical books and came across some charts of the human anatomy. For no apparent reason, she chose that moment to sit me down on the white couch and explain to me the internal workings of the sexual organs. And then I fainted and she had to use old-fashioned smelling salts to revive me. I fainted because her description was so medical as to be totally unrecognizable as a discussion about sex. Actually, I already knew all about sex. But over time, as this story is retold, she was just telling me the plain ol' facts of life and that's what caused me to faint. I no longer refute the claim, nor refuse my sisters their pleasure. (From the lawn chairs that first day, I can look around and see different parts of the ranch that remind me of things: the corral, the place where I had a garden, stuff like that. My sister Judith had brought her movie projector with her from home, and had decided to attempt to show the old home movies tonight. We haven't seen them very often. The few times my father tried to do this with his old 1950s projector, the projector would start burning up the film after a few reels. Tonight it works better, since Judith's projector is thirty years newer.) (And then talk about some scenes you see in the films and let my mom make a few comments about them. She might say something like, "You were a good baby. You were always good babies, but if you had colic I always felt guilty...") [*Tape ends.*]

How I Came to Dinosaur Pond

I was born in Los Angeles, California, in a hospital by the beach. I never forgave my mother for not having me at home in the white cement house we lived in next to the strand. It has a wooden swing set in the backyard and stairs, and it was divided into two families' homes. We had a two-tone plastic TV set my father won in a raffle. I like this house. I remember standing on the beach late one night with my sister. It was Halloween and she had on a gypsy costume and I don't know what I was, although I usually was a ghost at that age, about two, and my sister four, and we were all alone and it felt good. I always remember this.

We moved around L.A. beaches like Jim Morrison. We moved north to a run-down house in the country. A neighbor sold my father a cow and he named her after my mother. The cities were gone now for a while. I took long walks in the hills and woods by myself. I loved exploring slowly and lying for hours in secret places by a creek. My family all watched television together at night. Television was good then, and it fed us until we passed between sheets at night. On this little place I could have animals. I would talk to the little dog we got in the mountains for hours. I cried a long time when she ate cyanide somewhere and died. I have hated trappers ever since. I have always had a difficult time distinguishing between fantasy and reality. I make up things and later I don't know whether it has really happened or is something I made up. Sometimes I think the experience has really happened to me but somewhere else than here.

The first year I went to school I was very shy. The second year, I became very sarcastic and everybody liked me. Later, we would play games that I wasn't good at and then some people liked me less and teased me. I have always been clumsy, although I am capable of great grace and am usually quite graceful between clumsinesses. I went to school; I became very mental. I was political at an early age and very emotional about my politics. I was sexually attracted to women by my fourth year, although I had a great crush on Robert Horton from *Wagon Train*. I had a great ability to get along with most people while really liking only a few. I wanted to grow up fast and I wanted to never grow up.

Soon I became psychedelicized. It started with The Beatles, The Mamas and the Papas, pop music, dancing. I dressed like a hippie and now I had heroes. I painted, and had a girlfriend who was a better painter. We entered junior high and went crazy together. We talked a lot about love, and suicide. People thought the way we looked and things we were interested in strange. They liked us and elected me president. Then, very soon, they hated us. We stayed up late at night to write letters to each other and listen to underground radio. We had only each other. We didn't kill ourselves. She came close. We talked about having a baby and revolution and San Francisco music.

I started drinking big bottles of beer and wine with a friend I had but never made. I always wanted to make him but I never told him so and I never really did but I wrote a poem about it this year.

Now I couldn't stay home for any length of time and when I was home I had to be by myself. This was an absolute requirement to keep me from hurting myself. I hitchhiked constantly. I smoked a lot of marijuana and ate any kind of prescription pills I could find. Rosemary got caught smoking dope in the bathtub. Her parents had caught us in her bedroom once when they were supposed to be away but came home and they always hated me after that. I went to a million concerts with her, and my other friend, or both. I became a good panhan-

dler as I would become a good lot of things. I learned all
about drugs and how to sell them. I learned how to steal
from liquor stores. I learned how to lie my way into and
out of what I needed. Still I was gentle and my heart
ached when I saw someone hurt someone else. My heart
shut off when people hurt me.

I played football for a team at school, and that and
selling drugs made me very acceptable to a large group
of different people. People stopped hating me and liked
me some, even though they didn't know me. Not at all.
Rosemary was frightened. We would stop being lovers
while we were lovers with others and then we would be
lovers again. It was all very private with us and no one
ever knew what state our relationship was in and
sometimes we didn't know what we wanted to do
together on the outside and we knew each other more
than anyone should on the inside.

I started taking lots of psilocybin and LSD and lots of
times I'd be buzzed out at school all day. I had several
older friends I sold dope with and two of them took
heroin. They were both very pretty people, and very
gentle too. I became good friends with an older woman
who was pregnant and beautiful. We panhandled
together and then she would drive me around while I
drank or got stoned. She was getting very big and had
taken a lot of drugs all the time but wasn't anymore
because of the baby. She was afraid the baby would be
deformed. It wasn't, it was so beautifully featured and
soft, but it had something wrong with its heart. I would
try to hit telephone poles with empty bottles as we drove
along. All at night. Once she raced a train and we were
almost hit. She was a '52 Chevy. She wasn't crazy. I was.
I was still fifteen.

Then my old friends graduated and I felt alone at
school and I stayed with Rosemary and my other friend
a lot and I had some love affairs. One was with a girl
with big breasts who turned me on more sexually than

Sam D'Allesandro

any woman has since. I stayed up late reading Jerry Rubin and the Berrigans. My friend and I put up flyers about revolutionary struggle at the school. I collected money for Angela Davis. I was attracted to her. Once Rosemary helped us jam the school's switchboard and the panel started smoking and blew up. We stole mercury from the bio-lab when Mr. Pfeiffer turned his back for just a moment. We played with it, rolling little balls, while stoned, and buried it in an orchard. My father and I could only argue now.

I made a new friend with a woman—I was learning guitar now—who loved LSD even more than me. We sold drugs together. We started going on ski trips with this church youth group and we'd take psychedelics in the snow. Once I didn't go and the bus crashed and she was killed. I stopped talking to people for a long time. The newspaper wrote on the front page for weeks about a river of blood running down the road from the bus. They would not let me forget how mangled the bodies were. I tried to communicate with her at the funeral.

I started staying out all night and disappearing to San Francisco for long periods of time. My parents always thought I was staying with my friend. I stayed a lot in the Haight until the junkies started making everything harder. Berkeley became easier for a while. Now I knew the streets well and how to live on nothing and get drugs. I loved Janis Joplin.

I started reading the Bible after my friend died. I loved Jesus because he loved loving. Rosemary's parents kidnapped her and took her to Kansas. We wrote all the time. I had a Christian girlfriend for a while. I took lots of LSD by myself late at night and told my Christian friends how sacred this drug was, and they told me drugs would take all the power in my life. I did have a hard time staying away from drugs when I tried to, but they never took all my power. LSD gave me new power, I told them; the expanded mind could know God. I said

The Wild Creatures

we are all God on the inside and have to throw off our outer layers of conditioning and occupation to get to this place of being, a pure extension. I said all creation is sacred. I said all religions are blessed. I said it's time to change big and fast. I started having a lot of trouble at this church, so I left it.

A summer came where I didn't work and by the end of it I stayed home a lot. I would go out very early each day in an old rowboat we had, and drift naked on the pond. We had made a large wooden raft that stayed in the middle, and sometimes I would stay on that, lying in the sun all day and my mind would drift far away. I moved on a warm wind, that always came from inside me, to new and powerful lands. I soared for hours like an eagle in quiet skies. It was always quiet and peaceful. I could come back to the house for dinner and talk to no one, just "yes" and "no" to questions. Sometimes I could read and sometimes I would love to drink beer in the warm nights with an older friend I had. I used to sing to him because he loved my imitations of Janis Joplin. These were the only things I could do during this time. Somehow school began and someone would put me on the bus or drive me in a car and I would be there. Slowly I started coming back into contact with the outside world. I didn't want to. It happened gradually and I couldn't stop it. It was like a balance scale. At first, most of the day's hours were spent inside me. Then more and more hours spent in the outside world until I was there most of the time. I began to talk again and to hang around instead of really being somewhere, and even to listen to what people said. I took a huge dose of LSD to try and reverse this process. It happened very bad, and very black. I was alone and I couldn't move from this couch. I huddled and waited and waited for the LSD to end. I felt dead but I knew I wasn't, because I was still able to wish I was. Now there was nothing I could count on. I stopped taking psychedelics and drank a lot. I gave

Sam D'Allesandro

in to dulling reality, in despair of breaking through.

I began to work at night. I told the school I worked in the afternoon and since my grades were high in literature and art they let me go at noon. I could do history too. I could never do math, but I tortured myself with it anyway. In my last year of school mornings, I painted and took photographs. My photographs won some prizes. I painted an apocalypse, Leonard Bernstein (everyone thought it looked like Johnny Cash, so I gave it to my mother), Zachariah, more. I even painted Ali MacGraw. I wasn't patient. I used my hands when I painted. My art teacher loved me, let me do what I wanted, was criticized unmercifully, and went crazy. She had to leave the next year.

I met a woman teacher who agreed to teach me psychology. There was no class, just she and I. I read some books. Mostly we would sit and talk. She was interested in me. I could tell her things I couldn't talk to other people about and she wouldn't laugh. Sometimes we laughed together. Now I knew that having a friend didn't always mean torture and hiding. One day she let me borrow her car. I needed a car. She just gave me the keys. I'll never forget that. I started to feel like someone good. I graduated stoned and sucked up a bottle of champagne in a red Mustang. At five in the morning, Tim and I crawled through a fat older girlfriend's bedroom window and we all slept together.

After a while, I went to a college in the foothills. Suddenly there were others like me. I made friends. People wanted to be friends. Those people liked art and all kinds of music and the mountains. I met Marianna and she taught me yoga for over a year. I would go to her house and we'd swim naked together. She was so sexy. We often talked about sex and she told me about her ex-husband. I had a class with him. He was jealous of my friendship with Marianna and acted cold toward me. He still loved her. Later another professor told me that Joe

The Wild Creatures

liked my work. I was attracted to him. I loved Marianna. She and yoga helped me open my life and come outside. One night in class I was doing a yoga posture when I felt like my whole body was being electrically shocked. I passed out and shook. My eyes were filled with wonderful psychedelic spirals, like going inside the molecular structure of a molecule. Part of the shell had lifted.

I lived with friends and we played electric guitar together. We made tapes late at night using the instruments as free-form agents. We used African drums on the tapes. I met hippie women with long hair and full bodies. They were attracted to me. They liked my gentleness, so I became very gentle, like a sexual angel. I'd become a man and hadn't noticed, when I noticed in bed how thick and firm I was against women's softness. When I was hot, I wore almost nothing. Sensual enjoyment was the main priority. Suddenly it was good to be in my body. We swam naked in the rivers and danced to bluegrass-acid bands at night. We used to rub the tops of our heads together. There were cheap broken-down bars near my house. I went to one where Hell's Angels and hippies went wild together. Once I broke a bottle over someone's head there. They brought in bands and never checked IDs. We drank beer from the pitcher.

My landlord, Adolph, owned the bar and had a hotel in the upper stories of the building. I lived in another house he owned. The hotel was called La French. I had to go up sometimes to pay my rent. It frightened me. The halls were dark and dirty and the sleaziest people I've ever seen always hung around in the doorways. One night Adolph burned the building down to collect the insurance. That was the end of my favorite bar. I studied psychology and literature. In the spring I made films. I loved my people.

I became lovers with a woman who was older than me and divorced. I couldn't believe she loved me. She kept telling me that all the parts of myself and all my

Sam D'Allesandro

feelings were okay to have. I'm still learning this. She taught me to meditate. In the summer she went to school in the east. I went to Arizona and hallucinated in the Grand Canyon. I climbed to the bottom and watched the sides melt into a river of rock flowing down the trail to me. I read Yogananda. I came back to stay with Bruce. He was my best friend and we had lived together. We spent most of our time together, laughing and learning about making our own karma rules. Once we performed an exorcism on Friday, the possessed Dalmatian we lived with. Bruce and I were like lovers. People always said our names together. Sometimes we slept together. We made up medleys we would sing together: *Paint Your Wagon*, Neil Young, Yes. I had never been given so much unconditional love from another man before.

We went to Mexico—deep into the south. At first I was frightened and didn't know why. Then I learned that the earth would support me. I met old Mexican women Buddhas. I lived on a hut on the beach for fifty cents, swimming in the warm ocean. At night we'd watch stars and sometimes drink beer with the American girls from the one hotel. I didn't like the girls very much.

I came back to America. My first night I stayed with an old roommate, Moon. We slept in his big bed and in the middle of the night started touching. A new part of me was free. I had always loved men's bodies. Now I found I could touch them and love them too. Bruce and Moon and I found a new house in Chapman Town—the rural ghetto. We grew vegetables and had chickens. A million people came and stayed with us. Without words, a tribe formed. A woman stayed with me after a party and then didn't leave for a month. I fell in love with a man, and she went crazy. I couldn't stop events. People began to fight. Bruce and I fought, and the tribe of a million pieces split into a thousand directions. I had a place in several of those directions but I felt numb. It was the first time to watch a beautiful thing I helped create in

152

The Wild Creatures

this new life, separate from my adolescence and family, disintegrate and die.

I fell in love with Doug when I was nineteen. He was thirty, blond, rich, and bent. He was the most beautiful man I had ever seen. A blond angel with muscles and soft fur. We became friends. I went to his house for wine. He asked me to stay. I didn't think. I took off my clothes and turned out the lights. I didn't know if I was homosexual. I only knew I was in love with Doug more than I'd ever loved anyone before. My heart was in sweet pain from the fullness of feeling. Now he was my life. His family was rich, and he was very spoiled by having always been so handsome and moneyed. Everyone we met was attracted to him. He showed me good art and wine. I learned of quality that sometimes only the rich know. Now I knew the difference between my mother's towels and his towels. I didn't care. I just knew.

Doug affected me and gave me affection. He decided to leave his lover in San Francisco, who he owned the house with. I was afraid. I went to Canada and Montana with my brother. We saw grizzly bears in the back woods and I decided to hitchhike to New York. It took me three days. The Weather Underground bombed a building near the YMCA I stayed at in Philadelphia. I stayed with a friend setting up a photography studio in Greenwich Village. We lived two doors down from Marcel Duchamp's place. My friend Randy had photographed Baryshnikov and had dreams about him at night and he told Baryshnikov about the dreams. We slept together. He was very handsome and very neurotic. He had a huge cock. It was hard staying together. The heat was oppressive. I went to art museums or helped him during the day. At night I went to the ballet. Once I was his guest at an introductory EST seminar and got in a fight. Once I climbed the Statue of Liberty. From our bed, I could see the lights of the Empire State Building. I took cocaine. I remember sitting up all night in a loft in Soho, talking to this disc jockey for an underground radio station—the only one in New York, he said. He was underground because he was obscene. It was a beautiful night. Randy was upset about something. I didn't listen to him complain on the way home. Later I learned to take heroin. I started becoming addicted. I left for California.

I moved into a house in the middle of an orchard with people I didn't know. Doug and I once made love in the orchard because I was afraid for the people I lived with to know. Later I moved back to Chapman Town with good friends. My dependency on Doug began to ease. I studied art and was a teacher at a day-care center. I made new friends.

I fell in love with a woman I met at work. We would go dancing. We went to the coast. She had a three-year-old son. She taught me about macrobiotics. I learned what a mother was like when she was also a woman and a lover. Now I had a family. I found out how much people respect that, how much safer they felt around me as a strong hippie with a family, instead of a homosexual. I was also a homosexual. Doug and I remained lovers. I felt more relaxed, life slowed down, I was happy. I tested LSD in the mountains by a waterfall. It had been two and a half years since my bad trip. The blackness was gone. I saw God everywhere. One time I came back from the falls on LSD and went to visit my parents. My little brother threw some clothes at me at one point and said to put them in the laundry. I did it and my mother asked why and I told her, "Because he's God." She said, "Oh honestly!" I told Doug, and he didn't want to know. I told Sharon, and she knew and went back to being a mother.

I decided to move to Santa Cruz to go to the university. None of my past would be there, only what I brought. I wanted to be near the ocean. The ocean had always been my baptism, purger of my pain and re-

The Wild Creatures

newer of my spirit. By now I had another yoga teacher besides Marianna, Baba Hari Dass. He lived in Santa Cruz. The first time I saw him, I had hitchhiked down and I still had my pack on my back and tears rolled down my face. When I told Doug I was going, he decided to sell his house and go to Africa. I finally realized that he really did love me, in spite of our stormy relationship. The day I moved, he helped me load my truck. Sharon made me a lunch to take. I cried on the way and didn't know why I was going.

I lived near the sea with three women. First, I became lovers with a rich Australian girl. Then we stopped and I was gay. I met a lot of gay people for the first time, and a lot of other people who didn't care about being gay. People liked me. This time there was no tribe. There was me, with friends. Sharon visited. I made a bed with legs that sat high off the ground. Sharon's son would sleep in the little cave we made underneath. Doug came a few times before Africa. My friends could always tell when he had left by the way I looked. One would hold me and only then would I cry. I always cried. I felt I had overemphasized my angelic side as a hippie-yogi for too many years. It had become a new mask. I found I was also the devil. I loved my anger. I found I had to go to hell before I would reach heaven.

I learned how to be a scholar. My intellect was enforced. I became very opinionated. I knew how to stir things up. I felt a vendetta against false trappings of psychic comfort and meaningless clichés. I raged against the tyranny of the dull mind. Experience was to be in focus, sharp and strong. I went to the baths in San Francisco once. I met a very strong blond man and we became lovers. His name was John. He opened me up sexually. I found sex was not just an extension of love but could also allow me to become the expression of my throbbing energetic core. I found the total union of flesh to be holy. I stayed with John for six months. We never could talk. I took money I had saved when I raised sheep and flew to London.

I lived in Paris and Berlin and spent the winter on a beach in southern Crete. I lived with a blonde woman. We swam every day. The village where we were had nothing, no stores, no restaurants, no roads. An old man fed us for about two dollars a day. He liked us. We liked him. He always tried to feel up Dee under the table. I remember the way the wind whistled in the mountains at night. When I'm in quiet places, I still remember how powerful and strong it felt. I went all over Europe with different people. I met up with Doug for a while in Spain. I long to return to Berlin and Italy. In the Alps, I walked for days. I walked on high trails with white clouded nothingness below. I met the void. I met my fear. I surrendered ultimate power to the void. In Athens, I worked at a guesthouse called the Ferry Transport. I sold my blood to get enough money to go back across Europe to London. I went in a Magic Bus in the winter and I had pneumonia. I became friends with a scruffy, short, macho Scotsman, who took care of me. I wrote *Found Rhinestones,* my book of European poetry, the European working. I named it after my own actions. While I was traveling, I picked rhinestones out of a brooch I had, and threw them on the ground for children to find.

I stayed in New York awhile. Then I drove back to California through the South. I stayed in cheap hotels with this strawberry blonde I met in Switzerland. She drove me crazy. I liked looking out the window. I came back to San Francisco. John, my lover I met at the baths, took drugs all the time. He couldn't get a hard-on very often anymore. There was always heroin or something on the kitchen table. I moved to the mountains in Boulder Creek with my friend Mark. We wrestled and played and slept together. We weren't lovers. We had the most fun.

The Wild Creatures

Sharon and her son died in a car wreck. I remembered how she always loved me no matter what I did. I remembered how strong she was, how she took care of her son. I talked to her in the dark. I looked at a da Vinci on the wall, the *Madonna on the Rocks*. It was Sharon. I felt small and blessed. I went to school some and got a job as a counselor. I became friends with a German I met at a Patti Smith concert. He had on a black T-shirt and black eyeliner. He went to New York while I was in Europe, and he came back to Santa Cruz for a month and we became lovers. We went to New Orleans. We moved to San Francisco. Now I nurture art and loneliness. Life's gotten fast. I've gotten strong. I got a Detroit T-shirt. I met Sally Mutant. I picked up a New York lover. I got beat up in a New Orleans hotel room, and fucked more times than anyone needs to. I don't want to be a businessman. I can't think of a profession that doesn't bore me, so I do a number of jobs. They allow me to write and take pictures. I go out all the time and stay out late. I take drugs but they're not big in me. I'm an outlaw from social expectation, violent and violently romantic. I'm figuring out my own way. I'm more interesting than anyone I know — that's the way it should be. I live on the soft white underbelly of the city. I'm not addicted to happiness. I pursue feeling myself living. I worship a new icon, the dog with wings, god of fun and teenage integrity. I've regressed to about seventeen years old. I guess I got it together pretty good.

Kevin Killian is a poet, novelist, critic, and playwright. He has written a book of poetry, *Argento Series*, two novels, *Shy* and *Arctic Summer*, a book of memoirs, *Bedrooms Have Windows*, and two books of stories, *Little Men* and *I Cry Like a Baby*. For the San Francisco Poets Theater, Killian has written thirty plays, including *Stone Marmalade* (with Leslie Scalapino) and *Often* (with Barbara Guest). His next book will be all about Kylie Minogue.

Sam D'Allesandro, born Richard Anderson in 1956, studied at the University of California, Santa Cruz, and came to San Francisco as a youth in the early 1980s. He was handsome and charismatic, the man who'd turn your head at a hundred yards. He began as a poet and published a book of elegant lyrics called *Slippery Sins*. Soon he fell in with the so-called "New Narrative" writers Robert Glück, Bruce Boone, Steve Abbott and others, and his writing took a sharp turn toward an extreme purity and poise. He reached out to other like-minded writers and contacted Dennis Cooper, Kathy Acker, Benjamin Weissman, David Trinidad, and Dodie Bellamy, with whom he began an epistolary collaboration she was later to publish as *Real: The Letters of Mina Harker and Sam D'Allesandro*. At the peak of his powers, he began to feel ill. He died of AIDS in 1988, leaving behind a brilliant body of work that ranges from stories of one paragraph only to fully developed novellas.